I0563391

The Breaking Cage
Constance Pennington Smythe
Copyright © 2008
ISBN 978-1-934446-25-6
Cover Design by Sklaven

Published by
Romance Divine LLC 2008
Find us on the
World Wide Web at
www.romancedivine.com

Dedication

For my special girls.

You know who you are.

"PUT THAT BOOK DOWN! HAVE YOU FINISHED YOUR CHORES? NO, I DIDN'T THINK SO. GET ME MORE COFFEE AND THEN YOU CAN FINISH THE BREAKFAST DISHES AND START THE DUSTING.

"MASTER WILL BE HERE AT TEN AND YOU'RE GOING TO WASH AND WAX HIS CAR. OF COURSE YOU HAVE TO WEAR THOSE CUTE PINK SHORT-SHORTS AND CROP TOP! YOU LOOK CUTE IN THAT OUTFIT. DO A GOOD JOB ON MASTER'S CAR AND YOU CAN READ SOME OF MS PENNINGTON'S NEW BOOK BEFORE BED TIME."

The Breaking Cage

Constance Pennington Smythe

One

Karin Calloway relaxed in her chair and absently turned the pages of a magazine as the warm water and heated stones in the foot-bath soaked away the stresses of her day. Scents of vanilla and lavender filled the air; sconces on the wall gave the room a muted amber glow. The New Age music in the background, harps and flutes, that was something she could do without. Some vintage Sinatra, Old Blue Eyes with the Nelson Riddle Orchestra, or maybe even some Harry Connick Jr. would be more to her liking; elegant and classy as herself.

She watched a petite spa technician in a too-tight, too-short white dress administer a pedicure to another customer. She'd noted the girl's name badge, Tammy, when she'd started the footbath. Karin's eyes couldn't help but linger on the taut fabric as it stretched over those young, firm hips. *VPL, a fashion no-no, but there's something about her.*

The woman receiving Tammy's attentions was close to Karin's age and quite striking. Their eyes met when Karin entered the room and they exchanged polite smiles and nods in silent greeting. Then they both went back to their magazines and moments of selfish indulgence and pampering.

"Almost finished, Ma'am, your feet didn't need that much work. You're very fortunate to have a husband who takes care of them," Tammy said.

Karin raised her eyes and glanced over the top of her magazine, intrigued by the conversation.

Tammy turned to Karin. "I'll be right with you Ms. Calloway." She gathered up her things and prepared to move to Karin when the other woman spoke.

"Tammy!"

Tammy turned to face her client, who silently pointed to her feet.

Karin dropped the magazine, her terrycloth robe enfolding the pages. Something was going to happen and she didn't want to miss it.

Tammy stepped before her customer, knelt and reverently placed a tender kiss on the top of each foot. She released the feet and looked up to see the woman smiling down at her, but silently demanding more. Tammy picked up the pan of water from the footbath, brought it to her lips and took a drink, her pink tongue licking the residue from her lips. The woman in the chair nodded approvingly. The ritual act of obeisance completed, Tammy rose, set the pan on a shelf and gathered her things. She cast an embarrassed look at Karin. "I'll be right with you Ms. Calloway."

Karin's eyes followed Tammy as she left, then she turned her gaze to the woman across the room.

The woman rose, tightened her robe, and walked to Karin. "I hope I didn't shock you".

Karin smiled and shrugged her shoulders. "Actually, not at all."

"Really? Some would be shocked at such an overt and submissive display."

Karin's green eyes narrowed and she pursed her lips as if to consider. "Some would, ones who don't understand the desperate needs and nature of those who would be submissive. She said your husband does your feet?"

"Yes, quite well in fact. But I also enjoy the pampering here. And," she said, casting her eyes to the door, "Tammy is such a treasure."

"I quite agree, she is - special," Karin said, extending a hand. "My name is Karin Calloway."

"Joanna, Joanna Barnes," said the other woman, taking Karin's hand and smiling. "We really must get together."

Joanna added cream to her coffee. "I've not seen you at the spa before."

Karin dabbed at her lips with a napkin and returned it to the table. "Yes, I usually go to Giovanni's, but they're remodeling. Based on the performance of your lovely little Tammy I may consider switching locations. You noticed her submissive nature right off?"

"Not immediately, but even at the first appointment there was definitely something about the way she touched my feet, almost a - reverence."

Karin nodded. "Not surprising, someone with a strong submissive need couldn't help but exhibit some of that on the job, kneeling, giving pedicures, serving and waiting. She probably chose that vocation specifically for those reasons. How far have you taken her?"

"Only what you witnessed, foot kissing and drinking my footbath."

"Still, it makes for a wonderfully entertaining afternoon."

"Most entertaining."

Karin leaned back and considered her next question. "You said your husband does your feet. Is he submissive?"

"He likes to be dominated." Joanna paused, unsure how much to reveal to her new-found friend. "Get tied up and spanked. It was a bit of a shock at first, but as I got more comfortable with it I began to see it in more places. I saw the same look in Tammy's eyes that I'd seen in my husband's and out of curiosity I pushed it to see how far she'd go. I enjoy it: the power of having someone submit to me."

"How far have you gone with your husband?"

"Some bondage, foot kissing, he's bought crops, whips and paddles that I use on him."

"Uh-huh, sounds typical." Karin studied Joanna for a moment and leaned forward; here was new blood, a potential convert to the sisterhood. "How far would you like it to go?"

Joanna shrugged, having never considered the question. "I don't know. How far is there - to go, I mean?"

Karin's lips curled into a demonic smile, time to seal another submissive's fate. "All the way, complete submission to you, 24/7, or whenever you desire, complete service, absolute obedience. Admittedly it's not for everyone, but there can be some advantages - for you."

"I'm not sure." Joanna drummed her nails on the table nervously. "I can't imagine what that would be like. Even if it's something that I wanted – I mean; would Gary want to go that far?"

"That's your first mistake..." Karin settled back in her chair allowing Joanna some space, "...allowing him a choice in the matter."

Joanna hesitated. "I don't know, up until now it's been..."

"Would you like to see how it can be, how far it can go?"

Joanna silently nodded.

"Come see me on Friday...alone."

"HMM, LET ME GIVE IT SOME THOUGHT, MY PERSONAL 24/7 SUBMISSIVE. AND YOU CAN SHOW ME HOW TO MAKE THIS HAPPEN?"

"ABSOLUTELY. I HAVE A SYSTEM. BELIEVE ME, YOUR LIVES WILL CHANGE."

"I'M DEFINITELY INTERESTED."

Two

Joanna steered her BMW up the driveway, excited at what she might learn that evening. Karin promised to show her real dominance and submission, and Joanna was curious.

The dulcet tones of the doorbell had barely receded before the carved mahogany door opened. Joanna was greeted by a tall maid who demurely admitted her into the spacious and richly decorated foyer. The maid curtsied. "Welcome to Mistress Karin's home, may I take your coat?"

Joanna allowed the maid to take her coat and took the moment to observe the domestic help. Karin's maid was tall, as she'd noticed, but that was obviously due to the high stiletto heels that were part of the uniform. *They must be at least five inches high* thought Joanna.

The maid wore the classic black and white knee-length dress with white apron and lace headpiece on her shoulder-length brown hair. She gently folded Joanna's coat over her arm. "Please follow me."

Joanna followed, noting the maid's short steps, each foot directly in front of the other, providing a pleasing sway to her delightfully full and rounded bottom. She noted Karin's exquisite décor: Flemish tapestries, French tables with delicate vases and fresh flowers provided an Architectural Digest ambience that was more elegant than ostentatious. The woman had style.

When they reached the study, the maid curtsied and announced, "Ms. Joanna Barnes to see you, Ma'am."

Karin rose to embrace Joanna. "I'm delighted you could come." She turned to the maid, "I'll call for you when I need you."

Joanna noted Karin's curt and authoritative tone and watched as the maid executed a series of demure curtsies and backed out of the room.

Karin motioned to the sofa and both women sat down.

"Your home is stunning," gushed Joanna.

"I'll give you the tour later. It's so good to have you visit. Have you thought about our discussion? Are you curious to see how far dominance and submission can go in a relationship?"

"Yes, I am. You've definitely got me interested."

Karin smiled, "I'm glad. There's a wonderful world that awaits you, if you're up for taking it."

"I certainly wouldn't mind being pampered and treated like a Goddess if that's what you mean."

Joanna laughed and swept her arm around to indicate Karin's lifestyle. "So is your husband, your submissive, around? I'd like to see what it is you're talking about."

"Darling," cooed Karin, "you've already met him."

'I have? Where?"

Karin lit a cigarette and exhaled a stream of smoke. "He let you in. Suzette, the maid, is my husband."

"Get out!"

With an evil, Cheshire-cat grin, Karin nodded. "My complete submissive, docile, obedient and feminized sissy maid. Every woman should have one, they're such treasures. Let's call her back." Karin picked up a crystal bell and gave it two shakes.

Immediately Joanna heard the same click-clacking of stilettos she'd heard when she followed the maid down the hallway.

Karin's husband minced into the room, stopped before the seated ladies and executed a deep curtsey.

"Joanna, this is my husband and maid Suzette; more maid than husband aren't you, dear?"

Karin's husband delicately took the hem of his dress between his thumbs and forefingers, lifted it and dropped into another deep curtsey. "Yes, Mistress."

"Lift your dress," Karin ordered.

He lifted the dress to expose his cock, encased in a chastity device, and a lacy garter belt holding up his black, seamed fishnet stockings.

"Isn't she pretty?" mocked Karin.

Joanna stared, open-mouthed, slowly shaking her head. "Yes, quite feminine. Is - he always locked in that - thing?"

"Almost always," Karin replied. "It's really rather useless to me, unless I feel like tormenting or teasing her, which I quite enjoy. And keeping it locked up makes her more efficient in her duties, doesn't it, dear?"

"Yes Mistress."

"And do you always keep him dressed like this?" Joanna asked.

"Most of the time, actually her entire life, apart from her daily office job, is devoted to me, so at home she's nothing more than a servant, a maid, a domestic."

"He wears those heels all the time?

"Those are her day shoes. She wears higher ones, usually six inches or more, in the evening. And yes, she's in them all day and night when she's not at her male work."

Joanna furrowed her brow and bit her bottom lip. "You refer to him, or her, as she?"

Karin smiled and put a reassuring hand on Joanna's arm. "Yes, after training they seem to respond better to the feminine pronoun. Techni-cally they aren't really male or female, but rather sissy maids: domesticated, ultra-feminized males. Male references only confuse the poor thing. So, would you like to see where these darling little creatures come from, how they're born?"

Joanna took a deep breath and exhaled. "Love to."

"I was expecting something darker, more sinister, perhaps something medieval and dungeonesque," Joanna said, as they entered Karin's basement.

"That's the other side of the basement, my playroom. This is where I do my serious work, the life-changing work." Karin threw the light switch.

The room erupted into an explosion of light that made Joanna squint. It was clinically foreboding: cold white tiles on the floor, white walls and ceiling, and bright, harsh lighting. Karin picked up severe looking sunglasses, handing a pair to Joanna. "It frightens them more when they can't see our eyes. And the brightness in here can be disorienting, although the subjects are usually hooded." Karin slid on the sunglasses. "But there's no need for us to suffer." She jerked on the leash in her hand and Suzette dutifully crawled behind. Karin used her cigarette holder and casually pointed out features of the room, occasionally tapping an ash to the pristine white floor. Karin smiled as Suzette quickly lapped up each spot of gray ash. "Why bother with messy and smelly ash trays?"

The stark white walls, floor and ceiling were

punctuated with gleaming chrome and stainless steel. "No leather?" Joanna asked.

With a flourish Karin opened a cabinet revealing a wide assortment of cuffs, collars, hoods, gags, straps and arm binders. "Of course there's leather, there's always leather, darling, but I'm going for a more clinical look and feel here."

A tray of gleaming surgical stainless steel instruments caught Joanna's eye. She picked up a Speculum and squeezed.

Karin smiled to see Joanna's face light up with glee as the tool widened in her grip. She tugged on the leash and Suzette crawled behind, following Mistress to the center of the room. "And this - is the Breaking Cage."

Joanna silently eyed the nondescript assembly and pointed to a plaque. "What's that? What's **MISMO**?"

Karin jerked on the lead and Suzette heeled up at her side, her mouth open.

"That," Karin said, as she tapped the ash directly into Suzette's mouth, "stands for **Male In, Sissy Maid Out.**"

"Clever, but it looks like one of those portable dog cages."

"It is, darling, it is," Karin laughed, "but one with unique enhancements."

"What's that on the bottom of the cage?"

"It's a plastic mat for using office chairs on carpet. Only I've turned it over so the hundreds of tiny plastic spikes point upwards. It doesn't cause them any real damage, but it makes them uncomfortable. There's no position they can find where their knees and legs aren't tormented and assaulted. No relief, no comfort, it's all part of the programming and conditioning."

Joanna walked around the cage, intently observing its features, running her hand over the strong wire exterior. It was a heavy duty dog cage barely waist high. A male could be squeezed in, hunched over, on his knees, but Karin was correct; it wouldn't be comfortable. "So how does it all work?"

"Let me show you." Karin pulled on Suzette's leash. "Strip!"

Suzette's shaky hands struggled to remove her maid's dress.

"She's really scared," Joanna said.

"She has a right to be." Karin turned to her fearful maid. "I'm only putting you in for a quick demonstration, but if you give me any trouble I'll leave you there."

Suzette dropped to her knees to lavish thankful kisses on Karin's high heeled pumps.

Joanna shook her head. "She's scared shitless of that thing. Is that how you train all of them?"

"It's how I break all of them darling." Karin's lips parted into a wicked smile. "It's how we'll break yours."

Joanna nodded at the thought of Gary, bound and trembling, crawling into the cage. "Yeah..."

"Exciting isn't it?"

"Fucking-A right, show me how this thing works."

Karin began preparing Suzette for the cage. Suzette's arms were secured behind her with a leather arm-binder. Ear bud earphones were inserted into her ears. A leather hood with only a mouth opening rendered Suzette sightless and sealed in the earphones.

Karin turned a switch and flooded the room with static from a pair of JBL reference monitor speakers. She turned down the volume so she and Joanna could talk. "Random white noise, it's disorienting, makes it hard for them to think or concentrate and impossible to sleep."

Suzette's chastity device was left on and Karin affixed a metal band around the base of Suzette's scrotum. A wire from the metal band was connected to the same control panel where Karin plugged in Suzette's earphones.

Karin guided a shuffling Suzette into the cage, routing the wires through openings in the top. She positioned Suzette so she faced strategically placed doors that allowed access to her cock, tits and mouth. Karin pushed a button and a winch lifted the cage in the air. "I hate bending over to work, and the motion keeps them off balance and disoriented."

Karin began her discourse on the Breaking Cage. "What we have here are elements of sensory deprivation, sleep deprivation, behavior modification, and positive and negative reinforcement. The plastic cage bottom, white noise, cage motion and recitation drills deprive the inhabitant of rest, relief or rational thought."

"Recitation drills?"

"The very heart of the Breaking Cage, at random intervals the white noise is interrupted by a recorded statement. The subject must repeat the statement, aloud, within five seconds or suffer an electrical shock to the metal band around her scrotum, painful - but not damaging. Like this," Karin pressed a button and Suzette lurched in the cage.

"Aaaahggghhh!"

Joanna's eyes went wide. "What kind of statement?"

Karin's eyes narrowed to slits, made more mysterious by the haze of smoke from her cigarette. "The kinds of statements that turn men into sissy maids." She picked up a remote control and pressed PLAY.

From the speakers came a lilting female voice: "*I love to wear high heels.*"

Suzette replied without hesitation. "I love to wear high heels."

Again came the feminine voice. "*It's fun to wear makeup.*"

Just as fast came Suzette's reply. "It's fun to wear makeup."

Karin pressed STOP and the irritating white noise returned. "There are hundreds of such statements, computer controlled and which the subject is forced to hear and repeat for days on end. The subject's responses are monitored by computer. They go on, at random intervals, day and night - and if they're not answered, the subject gets an electric shock. Let me show you. I'll turn off the microphone that records Suzette's responses."

Karin pressed PLAY and the voice returned: *"I love to suck cock."*

Suzette's reply followed. "I love to suck cock."

Karin smiled and silently mouthed the word "wait."

The shock hit Suzette and she screamed in pain. "I LOVE TO SUCK COCK!"

Again she was shocked. "I LOVE TO SUCK COCK!"

Karin allowed one more shock before she turned on Suzette's microphone. "I LOVE TO SUCK COCK!!"

This time there was no shock and Suzette relaxed, although she was visibly shaking.

Joanna held her breath and leaned against a cabinet for support. "Un-fucking-believable. You do this for days?"

"For some it takes repeat sessions. For others, after two days there is absolutely no hesitation wear mascara, suck cock, or do anything else demanded of them."

"What about food and water? You said some of them are in here for days?"

Karin removed a large, realistic looking dildo from a drawer. "It's hollow inside and I put in a feeding mixture - oatmeal for carbs and tuna for protein - mixed up in a blender, not appetizing, but it contains the basic life-sustaining nutrients.

They learn to suck their nourishment through a cock or go hungry. I have another one for water, sometimes flavored with my own golden nectar or my lover's cum, just to get them used to the flavor."

Karin walked to the cage, lowered the door in front of Suzette's face and affixed the feeding cock. She picked up the microphone. "Feed!"

Suzette shuffled forward, the pointed plastic mat mauling her knees, took the cock in her mouth and rocked back and forth sucking the plastic phallus.

Karin opened the tit access door and caressed Suzette's nipples.

Suzette moaned, moved her tits closer to the cage and continued to deep throat the cock.

"She likes to have her nipples stroked," Karin said. "It's part of the conditioning; they learn to associate their own physical pleasure with sucking cock. We also do negative reinforcement, removing the hood and showing them pictures of themselves hunting or playing golf accompanied by electrical shocks.

"And this is how Steven became Suzette?"

"She was the first," Karin admitted. "I've done others, helping women create their own 24/7 domestic staffs."

Joanna eyed the caged feminized sissy maid contentedly rocking back and forth, hungrily feeding on the cock. "I want one, let's do it."

"COULD IT REALLY BE THAT EASY? TO TURN A MAN INTO A MINCING AND CURTSEYING SISSY MAID? I HAVE TO ADMIT; I LIKE THE IDEA OF BEING A PAMPERED QUEEN, MY EVERY WHIM FULFILLED. WHAT WOULD GARY LOOK LIKE IN A MAID'S DRESS? COULD HE LEARN TO WALK IN THOSE STILETTOS? DO I CARE? I JUST WANT IT TO HAPPEN. A SISSY MAID HUSBAND..."

Three

"*Nervous, baby?*" teased Joanna. His white-knuckled grip on the steering wheel told her more than any words.

Gary shifted in the driver's seat. "Yea, sure, a bit, aren't you?"

"Hey, baby, I'm not the submissive going to meet a lifestyle Dominant Female. But it's your fantasy, isn't it? I just want to give you what you want."

"Yeah, yeah, I guess so."

"We can turn back. If you can't go through with it we can always…"

"OK, OK! I'm doin' it. OK?"

Joanna fought back a smile. Karin told her that some nervousness on Gary's part was to be expected, that they could actually use that, play on it. She patted his knee. "Just do what you're told and don't speak unless you're asked. It'll be fine. Turn right at the next corner, sweetheart."

Gary was impressed, the large house was set well back from the street in a very upscale area. He parked the car next to a sleek Jaguar whose personalized plates read PURRRR.

He rang the doorbell and heard the deep tones of the bell echo through the house, followed by a faint clicking sound.

The door opened and Suzette curtsied. "Mistress Joanna, welcome to Mistress Karin's home. It's a pleasure to have you visit again."

Gary marveled at the maid as they were ushered into the house. He leaned to Joanna and whispered, "She has a maid and she remembers you."

"Yes, what do you think of that?" Joanna smiled, *if he's impressed with the house and the maid...*

Suzette curtsied again. "Mistress Karin is in the library; if you will please follow me." She turned on her stiletto heels and started down the marble hallway.

Suzette's heels clicked down the floor and Gary pointed at the frilly thing mincing before them. "Look," he whispered, "fishnet stockings with seams and spike heels. That's hot! Your new friend is really something."

"You like that?"

"Oh yeah, it's really sexy."

"Yes, isn't it," Joanna said. *That's good to know; I'm so glad you like that look.*

Suzette admitted them to the library, curtsied to her Mistress and announced the guests. Karin rose from her chair and embraced Joanna. "So good of you to come, please have a seat. That will be all Suzette; you may bring the refreshments when I ring for you."

Suzette nodded and backed from the room.

"And this must be Gary," Karin said as she and Joanna settled to the couch. "Do not sit!" Karin ordered as Gary started to take a seat. "Here, come and kneel at our feet."

Gary looked at Joanna who silently mouthed "do it" and watched as Gary fell to his knees.

"Much better," purred Karin. "Doesn't that feel good, kneeling before us?"

"Yes Mistress, it feels, uh - natural."

"He likes your maid," Joanna said. "He thinks she's hot."

"Does he now?" Karin chuckled. "Do you like to dress up?"

Gary shifted on his knees and blinked his eyes.

Karin crossed her legs, the seductive sound of the sensuous fabric drawing Gary's attention. "It's a simple question. Have you ever put on a pair of Joanna's panties? Well?"

Gary stared at Karin's high heels and mumbled his reply. "Yes, Mistress."

"Look at us when we talk to you. Are you wearing panties now?"

"Yes, Mistress."

"I made him put on a cute pair," Joanna said.

"Let's see," Karin said. "Strip, show us your

pretty panties - NOW."

Gary stood and quickly removed his clothes, folding them and placing them on a nearby chair. The women watched with detached amusement, laughing at his efforts to avoid eye contact. Within seconds he was naked, save for a pair of women's pink nylon panties. He resumed his kneeling position, a man exposed, stripped of his clothes, stripped of his masculinity and his pride. He was truly humbled.

Karin used the toe of her pump to kick his legs apart, exposing him even more. "Lovely panties, Joanna, pink is a good color for him. Do you like your pink panties?"

"Yes, Mistress."

Karin picked up a crystal bell and gave it three quick shakes.

Gary heard the clicking of heels on the floor and watched Suzette push a serving cart into the room and serve the women Champagne.

Karin snapped her fingers, "Suzette, come here and meet Gary."

Suzette walked up and stood before Gary, towering over him in her spike heels.

"Dress up!" Karin commanded.

Suzette delicately lifted her dress and Gary's eyes widened to see the plastic-enclosed cock hanging from Suzette's groin.

Gary turned to Joanna, "She's - it's a man!"

Karin cut the air with her crop, striking Gary's thighs.

He yelped, at both the pain and the surprise;

where had that come from?

"No unauthorized talking," Karin said.

Joanna was impressed with the way Karin seized control. "Suzette is Karin's husband - and maid. She's very pretty don't you think?"

Gary knelt, open-mouthed and silent, looking back and forth between Joanna and Suzette.

Again he felt the sting of the crop, the red welt blooming on his fair skin. Karin and her crop commanded his attention and he turned to her.

"Your Mistress asked you a question. Respond to her – politely."

He looked at Joanna. "Uh, yes, uh, Mistress, she is pretty."

"Would you like to be a pretty maid?"

"No, Mistress."

"But you're wearing women's pink panties aren't you? Don't you like to wear panties?" Joanna's eyes sparkled and the cruel smile that played across her lips was a sure sign that she felt the heady power of domination. "A few more things and you could be a pretty maid, just like Suzette. I think I'd like that. Don't you want to make me happy?"

Gary's eyes darted between Joanna, Karin and the feminized male, Suzette. He wasn't sure how to reply. What did they want?

"Look,' Karin said. "He's giving us his answer."

Gary followed their eyes to his crotch, his erection causing his pink panties to tent in the most humiliating fashion. He realized he was shaking – and erect. The beautiful and powerful women, his naked and kneeling body, and the pretty and sissified Suzette, all of this was exciting him, he was betrayed by his biology.

Joanna laughed at him, her mocking and lilting voice bringing him back to reality. "What is it darling, do you like being on your knees, or being hit with the crop, or kneeling before women, or do you want to be a sissy maid like Suzette?"

"Maybe it's all of that; I think all of this is turning him on." Karin used her crop to lift Gary's chin and look him in the eyes. "I think our little Gary wants to play with us like Suzette does. Do you want to be a pretty sissy maid and be bossed about by women?" Karin extended her leg, the silken, sheer stocking-clad appendage ending in an exquisite high-heeled pump.

Gary didn't even realize his head was shaking 'yes' as he bent forward to reverently kiss the toe of Karin's shoe.

While Gary lovingly worshipped Karin's high heels, Joanna and Karin toasted their Female Domination victory with Champagne. "Let the training begin," Karin said, punctuating her declaration with a slap of her crop to Gary's ass. "Stand up!"

Gary winced at the blow, but quickly stood as Karin continued to prod and poke him with her crop.

"Head down, eyes on the floor, hands clasped behind your back, feet apart - further."

Gary complied with each command, fighting the urge to look to see how Joanna reacted.

Karin continued, her imperious and matter-of-fact tone further objectifying Gary. "How you posture him is up to you. I'd recommend different stances for different things: a presentation position for inspection, a waiting position, a punishment position. Suzette, present!"

Joanna turned to see Suzette quickly assume the 'present' position. Suzette's feet were spread, her hands clasped behind her neck and her breasts thrust forward.

"Of course Suzette is fully clothed and the present position is best when they are naked. But you can see how it exposes their crotch," Karin used her crop as a pointer, "their titties, all their vulnerable areas."

Joanna looked Gary in the eyes. "Present!"

Gary tried his best to copy Suzette's posture, but he couldn't match the grace at which Suzette fell into the various positions and moves.

Joanna furrowed her eyebrows and placed her hands on her hips; disgusted at his clumsy efforts.

"He'll get better," Karin said, "repeated training, practice and discipline, and he'll improve." She turned to Suzette. "Down."

Suzette gracefully moved from 'present' to 'waiting'.

"Nice," Joanna said, "very smooth." She spun on her heel and slapped Gary. "And that's how you're going to learn to do it! Do you understand?"

"Yes, Mistress."

"And for now a little punishment; Gary needs to know the penalties for failure or poor perfor-

mance. Suzette, bring the discipline hammock."
Karin turned to Joanna. "Just a little tune-up,
something to send him home to think about."

"Whatever," laughed Joanna, "works for me."

Suzette pushed an elaborately upholstered
leather hammock to the center of the room. Gary
was placed face down, his stomach fitting nicely
onto the raised hump in the center. From the
bottom of the unit Suzette extended telescoping
steel rods from the four corners. Locked in their
fully extended positions they served as the anchors for the wrist and ankle cuffs Joanna and
Karin were affixing to Gary. When they finished
he was spread-eagled and tightly tethered: open,
exposed, helpless and vulnerable.

"What an innovative piece of furniture, I simply must have one," Joanna said.

Karin picked up a rattan cane and made practice cuts through the air. "Yes, it's quite handy,
I'll introduce you to the builder, he does some
amazing bondage furniture; you ought to see my
Ass Throne." Karin lightly rat-a-tat-tatted Gary's
bottom with her cane. "They need regular discipline, routine beatings to help them reinforce
their role in your dominant/submissive relationship. This is not punishment, that's reserved to
correct behavioral needs or punish them for er-
rors. I always make punishment sessions much
worse than discipline sessions so they know the
difference, both physically and cognitively."

"Shit," Joanna said, "there seems to be a lot
to all this, should I be taking notes?"

"No, it will come naturally, I promise." Karin held up the cane. "Used correctly, this will strike, no pun intended, fear into him at all times. It takes little effort to deliver pain and terror."

Karin took Joanna through Flagellation 101: floggers, cat-of-nine-tails, crops, canes and paddles, where to strike and pacing. "I usually gag them," explained Karin, "but I thought it best not to gag Gary today so you could hear the sounds and responses elicited by the use of each implement."

"Trust me," Joanna laughed, "it's been very educational."

Karin nodded. "His name, Gary, you need to change that and eventually start using the feminine pronoun with him. I've found it best to give them something girly. It helps with the conditioning."

"OK, I'll give it some thought."

Karin reached down and affectionately patted Gary as one might pet the family dog. "Have him take next Friday and Monday off and bring him here. We'll start with a long weekend in the Breaking Cage and see where we have to go from there."

"Do you think it's going to work?" Joanna asked.

Karin smiled. "Start shopping for the maid outfits, shoes and lingerie you want her to wear."

"I HOPE YOU ENJOYED OUR VISIT WITH KARIN AND SUZETTE. WE'RE COMING BACK NEXT WEEKEND FOR A LONGER VISIT. WHY SO QUIET, AREN'T YOU EXCITED? DON'T WORRY, BABY; I THINK YOU'RE GONNA GET ALL OF YOUR FANTASIES FULFILLED, AND MAYBE MORE."

Four

Joanna noticed a difference in their relationship the next week. Gary became quieter and more subdued as she found herself becoming more demanding. Their bondage and domination play took on a new edge with Gary quickly submitting to her every demand.

This wasn't all bad for Joanna who took advantage of her husband's new-found submission. She enjoyed foot rubs, massages and extended bouts of oral sex. Gary nestled between her legs while Joanna relaxed with a magazine, contentedly letting her husband kiss, suck and nuzzle at her womanly font of power. As necessary, she would grab his hair and pull his face into position to force his tongue into that sweet spot, or grind his nose relentlessly against her clit. She found herself easily falling into a pattern of using Gary as a sex object, a mere tool for her pleasure. Everyday she was on the phone with Karin, her new-found cohort in Dominance.

"I picked out the cutest little maid's dress, it's so frilly. He won't be able to wear it and retain a shred of masculinity," Joanna said.

"Darling, when we're through with him he'll want to wear it, can't wait to put it on. And as for masculinity, we'll remove any shred of that."

"I still need him to go to work; he has a job and career that brings in a good income. I don't want to send a simpering sissy to work everyday and risk losing his earning potential."

"Trust me Joanna, he'll go to work and bring that salary home - to you. From now on, it will be your money. But you'll find that he is much more careful about his appearance, his nails will be manicured, his hair perfectly combed, eyebrows plucked. You can put him in bras and panties, garter belts and stockings, pantyhose, anything you want under his male work clothes. The women and the gays that work with him will probably notice a change, but to the rest of the world, those other *males* he'll simply be a neat freak.

"And at home, he'll be my maid?"

"He'll be whatever you want him to be, but the cage and its training protocols are designed to create sissies, something decidedly feminine and subservient. He can be a maid, housewife, slut, stripper, schoolgirl, hooker, cheerleader, whatever will entertain and serve you and whoever else you want. Are you taking a lover?"

Joanna paused. "You know, I've started thinking about that. I do like all the foot worship and oral sex, getting my own way, but I think I'd miss having a man with a real cock."

"Darling, there's no reason you should ever be deprived of a good cock. You can even make Gary procure them for you, check out potential lovers, make your date and dinner reservations."

Joanna's chuckling on the other end of the phone brought a smile to Karin's lips. *Joanna and Gary will make a welcome addition to our circle.* "So you and Gary will be coming over this weekend, and we can begin his re-programming?"

"We're both looking forward to it, although Gary thinks it's going to be more of a Fem Dom scene session, whips and leather, boot licking."

"Yes - well, it will be a Fem Dom session, but not like anything he can imagine."

Joanna paused, behind her hazel eyes her mind was working out timelines. "How long do you think it will take, in the cage I mean, to change him?"

"They're all different, but most, especially if they have an inherent submissive nature, don't last long. We'll start with a long weekend, Friday evening through Sunday and see how he responds. In the meantime you can enjoy a weekend here with Suzette and I. I'll even arrange that cock you're longing for."

"Can you now?" Joanna laughed.

On Friday afternoon Gary took the single suitcase from the bed and carried it to the car. "Are you sure I'm not going to need anything? We'll be there all weekend." Joanna's icy look silenced him; the last few days her dominance had been ever increasing. Without another word he bowed his head, shut the trunk, and opened the passenger door while Joanna slid into the seat. He felt more like a chauffeur than a husband, exactly what Joanna intended.

Joanna decided a haughty silence would increase Gary's uneasiness, so she let Gary drive while she quietly smoked. She made a display out of crushing out her cigarette, her black, leather gloved hand slowly grinding the butt into the ashtray, as if the butt were Gary's manhood, being gradually broken and tossed away. "This weekend will be a test of your submissiveness. Mistress Karin has agreed to assist in your training and show us some of the finer points of dominance and submission. All you have to do is quietly submit and obey. You've met Karin's submissive, Suzette; simply follow her lead, she's been well trained."

Gary's reply was barely audible, a whispered, "Yes, Mistress."

"You do want this don't you? You've enjoyed our recent lifestyle haven't you?"

"Oh yes, Mistress, very much so."

"Good, remember, Karin is the real deal, it's not a game to her." Joanna reached over to tenderly stroke his cheek. "Do what you're told, don't speak unless you're spoken to and everything will be fine. Trust me."

"Yes, Mistress."

"I promise you, this weekend will fulfill all your fetish fantasies."

"Mistress, what about you?"

Joanna lit another cigarette, the action disguising the cruel smile playing across her lips. "I'll be getting everything I want, baby, everything."

"Joanna, how delightful to see you," Karin said as the two embraced.

Gary walked up with Joanna's suitcase, gently placed it on the ground, and dropped to his knees.

The two women stepped back from each other and smiled. Karin extended her foot, clad in a stylish high-heeled mule.

Gary placed his hands on the ground, leaned forward and placed a reverent kiss on Karin's shoe.

Karin quickly pulled her foot back. "Enough! Up! Suzette will show you to Joanna's room. Unpack her bag." She turned to Suzette. "Strip him and bring him to us when you finish preparing Mistress Joanna's room."

Suzette performed a low and delicate curtsey which Gary tried, with limited success, to emulate. Suzette minced away in her stilettos and Gary quickly picked up Joanna's bag and followed.

Karin took Joanna's arm, "Come, we'll relax and wait for them. Let me tell you about the cock I've found for you this weekend."

Suzette finished precisely laying out Joanna's makeup on the bathroom vanity, and stepped back to give it one last look. Satisfied, she entered the bedroom where Gary was putting the last of Joanna's clothes into a drawer. "Put the suitcase in the closet," Suzette said.

When Gary finished he turned to face Suzette. "Do you know what they're going to do?"

Her black page boy wig bobbed as Suzette shook her head 'no.' "Whatever they want, it's not for us to consider or think about. You need to remove your clothes, quickly; we mustn't keep the Mistresses waiting."

Receiving no further information or indication that additional info was forthcoming Gary started to remove his clothes.

"Everything," reminded Suzette, "even the panties. I like your pretty lacy panties."

"Yeah, uh, thanks." Gary handed over his clothes and slipped the pink panties down his legs.

"When we go in, don't look at them unless you're told to. Keep your hands at your sides. Don't speak unless you're asked a question and keep your answers honest, simple and respectful. Don't make any sudden moves; be elegant and graceful. They may inspect you, touch you, whatever. Let them and don't flinch." Suzette saw the worry in Gary's eyes. "Don't think about it too much. You'll fuck up, it's a given. Mistress Karin can make it happen at her will. And she'll teach that to your Mistress as well."

Suzette grabbed Gary's nipples, pulling, twisting and pinching them. "Makes them stand out a bit and gives them some color. Let's go, and take small steps, it's something you'll have to get used to."

"Well here they are," Karin mocked, "our submissive sissies."

Suzette led Gary into the room, stopped before Joanna and Karin, and executed her usual delicate curtsey. Gary ungainly tried to duplicate the move.

"Sloppy," Karin said. "We'll fix that, among other things." She turned to Suzette. "Put her on the curtsey trainer for fifty reps when we're through here."

"Yes, Mistress."

Gary grimaced as Suzette executed another one of her damned perfect curtsies. *What the fuck is a curtsey trainer?* He couldn't help but glance at Joanna and immediately the crop in Karin's hand lashed out, leaving a welt on his thigh.

"Eyes down slut!" Karin commanded.

He lurched at the blow, feeling the thin stripe bloom in pain. This was different from the bondage and discipline sex games played with Joanna. Karin was the real deal, a thought that both frightened and excited him.

"Didn't take him long to fuck up," Joanna observed.

"Never does," replied Karin, "they're all slow learners at first, but they do learn, some slower than others, but all painfully - for them." She turned her gaze to Suzette, who'd remained still, head down, hands demurely clasped behind her back, living proof of the efficacy of rigorous training. "We'll have supper in the dining room at seven. You and this worthless sissy here will serve. Lock a collar on it but keep it naked. And teach it to curtsey before supper! You're dismissed!"

Suzette and Gary both curtseyed and backed out of the room to the laughter of the ladies on the couch. Shaken and humiliated, Gary padded along on his bare feet as Suzette's spike heels click-clacked down the hallway.

Suzette stopped and ushered Gary through a door and down the staircase into the basement.

Gary descended into the dark abyss, his naked form shivering from the coolness. His eyes slowly adjusted to the dark as he exited the stairs and his feet touched the hard, cold tile floor.

"To the right," whispered Suzette, as she turned on a light switch.

Gary blinked as Karin's dungeon was bathed in light. It wasn't brightly lit; rather the electric lighting took the form of flickering candles casting shadows throughout the room.

Pausing, forgetting the chill of the room, Gary looked around, mesmerized by the many whips, paddles and crops hanging from the wall. A spanking horse and pillory took center stage in the room while an ominous cross and wheel adorned the far wall. Chains and manacles hung from various parts of the ceiling.

Suzette took his hand and pulled him across the room. "Over here, Mistress wants you to practice on the curtsey trainer."

In a daze Gary followed her, his eyes darting endlessly throughout the room, awed by the wicked splendor of Karin's dungeon. Suddenly he felt Suzette grab his nipple, violently pinching and twisting it.

"Pay attention!" she said. "We need to finish this and get back upstairs to start supper. Bend over."

Gary bent over and heard Suzette pull on a latex glove. He jumped as Suzette rubbed the cool lube around his puckered nether hole.

"Ever had anything in here?" Suzette asked.

"No, I'm not gay."

"Don't be silly," Suzette laughed, "it doesn't mean you're gay. And anyway, it's not your bottom; it belongs to Mistress Joanna, doesn't it?"

"I don't know, yeah, I guess so."

"Well, since this is your first time, we'll start with a small one on the trainer." Suzette's eyes closed as she slowly inserted one well-lubed finger and felt Gary gasp and lurch. "Easy precious, I'll go slowly. If you relax and breathe it will be easier on you. Now let me get some lube in there."

Gary tried to relax and breathe as Suzette slowly inserted a second finger. He shook with - what? Pleasure? Disgust? He'd never been violated in this way before and in all honesty he didn't know whether he liked it or not. When Suzette's other hand found and gently stroked his nipple he whimpered. He did like it, all of it.

"See there precious, not so bad is it?" cooed Suzette. She leaned down and kissed the back of his neck.

Gary was overcome by the sensations, as Suzette's nimble fingers coaxed waves of pleasure from his ass and nipples. Her soft lips on his neck, the scent of her perfume, the gentle voice had him melting in her arms. *But Suzette is a man, Karin's husband.*

"Yes, that's it baby, relax," Suzette mewed as she slowly withdrew her fingers.

Gary sighed as she pulled out.

Suzette pointed at Gary's throbbing erection, "I think you liked that. Maybe our Mistresses will allow us to play together sometime."

Utterly confused by this flood of emotions Gary silently looked at the raging hard-on between his legs. Wordlessly, he let himself be led to the curtsey trainer.

"The curtsey is a sign of respect. There are different ones to use at different times, but for now you will learn 'The Bob.' You can use this whenever Mistress enters or leaves a room you are in or to acknowledge an order you are given. Of course Mistress will dictate what curtseys you are to use and when." As Suzette talked she affixed a small butt plug to a metal rod protruding from the floor. "Stand here," she said, pulling Gary until he stood over the rod. "Put both feet on the ground with the pole between your legs. Your hands should be crossed in front of you." Suzette demonstrated the position and Gary followed. "Now bend your left knee, place your left foot behind the right foot, only keeping the toes of your left foot on the floor. Posture is very important, so keep your head up but your eyes down."

Gary copied Suzette's actions, assuming the same position she adopted.

"Very nice," complimented Suzette. "Next you need to bend at the knees and dip, lower yourself down until the plug goes into your bottom." Suzette giggled and slowly bent at the knees illustrating the proper curtsey. "Now you."

Slowly Gary bent his knees, stopping for a moment when his bottom touched the plug.

"It's not that big," chided Suzette, "and both

you and it are well lubricated. Now slowly, down and up."

With a deep breath Gary descended, the plug slowly sliding in and filling him, and then easing out when he stood.

"Back straight, don't bend forward at the waist, bend in the knees, down and up," corrected Suzette, "again."

Gary proceeded to curtsey, each time impaling himself on the plug. Suzette made minor adjustments on the plug height and position and by curtsey number fifteen Gary was starting to find the proper motion and technique.

"Be elegant and graceful, not stiff, no jerky movements." Suzette positioned Gary's body, helping him attain the correct posture. "Don't think about the plug in your bottom honey, focus on the movement. You want to be demure, sweet, something your Mistress can be proud of. Deeper sweetheart, get the plug all the way in, keep your back straight."

Gary lost count of the repetitions as he worked on his 'Bob' curtsey. He hoped that Suzette was counting; he wanted this to be over. When he finished the last curtsey his legs were beginning to cramp and his bottom was starting to hurt.

Suzette wiped the remaining lube from Gary's well-used ass. "Of course there are bigger plugs and your Mistress will probably make use of them. Eventually you'll have to learn all the types of curtseys and you'll be expected to perform them perfectly, all the time. Here," she said handing the plug to Gary, "there's a sink in the corner, go wash this off."

Gary held the butt plug in his hand; he felt its slickness and warmth. He wordlessly padded away on his bare feet while Suzette selected a collar.

When Gary returned Suzette held up a wide and stiff leather collar, emblazoned with the word 'SISSY' in sparkling crystals. "It's a posture collar."

Gary allowed Suzette to fasten the collar around his neck, securing it with a small padlock and attaching a leather lead to the front. Pulling on the lead, Suzette led Gary out of the dungeon, back upstairs and into the kitchen.

Karin savored the last of her Champagne and placed the glass on an end table. "We'll put him in the cage after supper."

Joanna silently nodded.

"Are you worried, having second thoughts?"

"No," Joanna said. "I'm good with it. No one is physically restraining him. He could get up and leave at any point. But he hasn't, he stays and obeys, no matter how we seem to treat him."

"It's his nature, Joanna, he wants to submit. He needs to revel in that sublime aura of Feminine Authority." Karin uncrossed her legs, the silk stockings sensuously rustling against one another and reached over to put a reassuring hand on Joanna's arm. "And we will take him to that place; that hallowed ground of male subjugation. I've seen his kind before; he'll be happy there, content to submit, obey and serve. Your relationship is going to change."

"I lose a husband and gain a maid."

Karin sat back and shrugged. "Well, technically, legally, on the marriage certificate he is still your husband. And depending on what you decide he will continue to be to the world at large. It's going to be whatever you want to make it."

"I can make this work, if you can deliver on that cock you promised."

"He'll be joining us after supper," Karin laughed. "Gary can meet him then."

Five

Gary followed Suzette about the dining room, amazed at the way she effortlessly moved on her spike heels. She kept up a running dialogue and Gary knew he'd never remember everything she said.

"The salad fork goes closest to the service plate, that's the big one. We're doing it that way tonight because we're serving the main course ahead of the salad. Sometimes it's done that way. The dinner fork is to the left of the salad fork and the fish fork is usually on the outside. But we aren't serving any fish tonight. The water glass, that's the large one, goes - "

"Don't you ever miss being a man?" Gary asked.

Suzette spun on a spiked heel, her head quizzically cocked to the side. She furrowed her brow and pursed her lips. "What a silly question! The water glass, the biggest one goes to the upper right of the setting with the white wine and the red wine glasses to right, in that order."

Gary wasn't going to get an answer to his question so he continued to follow Suzette throughout the dining room, trying as best he could to absorb her instructions. "Suzette, I'll never be able to remember all of this!"

She took his hand in hers and gently stroked his cheek with the other. "Of course you will honey, it will all be second nature to you, and everything you do will become automatic. It will be in your head, all the time, and when you need to know - you will. Mistress will make it happen."

"Happen, how?"

"You'll just know; it will be in your head. Now let's hurry to the kitchen and finish."

Suzette heard the tinkling bell and turned to Gary. "They're ready for supper, we need to go and meet them in the dining room. Follow me and do what I do."

Gary followed Suzette to the dining room, noting with interest how she took the time to fix her apron just so and adjust her maid's headpiece while she walked. The gestures seemed automatic. Gary couldn't believe that the uber-feminine creature mincing on the skyscraper heels in front of him had once been a man. Well, actually still was a man somewhere under all that feminine finery. *Does he play golf or have poker nights?*

Suzette entered the dining room taking a final quick look at the table setting before adopting her 'waiting' position by the door. Gary mimicked her stance: feet together, arms clasped behind the back, head and eyes down.

Karin and Joanna entered the room, the sharp staccato of their stilettos on the polished wood floor heralding their arrival. They proceeded to their places at the table, Suzette immediately falling in behind Karin and holding her chair out for her. Gary followed suit, performing the same function, albeit with less grace and elegance, for Joanna.

"It looks very nice," Karin said as Suzette delicately unfolded the fine linen napkin over her Mistress's lap.

Gary watched Suzette effortlessly execute the 'bob' curtsey and offer a "Thank you, Mistress."

"And how did your little helper do?"

"It's a good start, Mistress, it shows potential," Suzette said.

Gary recoiled to think of himself as an 'it'.

Joanna nodded her approval. "This is lovely; do you dine this way often? I could certainly get used to this kind of treatment."

"Oh yes, I enjoy this level of service quite often, it's one of the advantages of having a sissy maid."

"Bend down, let me see your collar," Joanna ordered. "SISSY, isn't that darling, you look so cute, naked with only your little collar." Joanna's hand snaked out to grab Gary's balls, making him jump as she clutched them. "Wouldn't you like to spoil me like this darling?" She squeezed harder.

"Yes, yes, Mistress."

Karin smiled as the husband/wife domination scene played out before her. "You may serve now."

The women enjoyed a laugh as Suzette and Gary left to bring in the meals.

"I now see what you mean when you told me that day that you could show me how it could be, how far it could go. You literally live like a pampered Queen."

"You haven't seen it all yet," Karin replied. "There's so much: massages, baths, shaving my legs, pedicures, waking me each morning with loving licks to my feet, not to mention cleaning house, shopping, laundry, errands, making dinner reservations for my dates, a warm tongue in my ass whenever I want it. It goes on and on."

"He tongues your ass?"

"It's heaven. I have a special chair built. When we get Gary squared away I'll have Suzette demonstrate for you. When was the last time you had a good orgasm from a tongue in your ass?"

"Hell, I guess never. Gary goes down on me sometimes. I don't think he's all that into it, but he does it to please me. But tongue my ass, never."

"Darling," Karin laughed, "your life is about to change for the better in so many ways."

Joanna shook her head in amazement. "Ok I'm all yours; teach me how to make it happen."

"For tonight simply follow my lead. Gary will

be doing whatever Suzette does."

The clicking of Suzette's heels and the dull flip-flopping of Gary's bare feet made the women look to see each submissive approaching with a plate of prepared food.

Serving professionally, from the right, Suzette bent her knees and offered the plate. Karin's subtle nod prompted Suzette to set the plate in front of her Mistress, back away and execute another small curtsey.

Watching this, Gary replicated the effort, placing the plate before Joanna and backing away to do the requisite curtsey.

Joanna couldn't help but laugh like a giddy schoolgirl. "They are so cute, so precious."

Gary blushed, embarrassed by both his nudity and at being referred to as 'cute and precious.'

When Karin snapped her fingers Suzette silently moved to Karin's right side and delicately dropped to her knees.

With a nod from Karin to do the same Joanna snapped her fingers and watched Gary obediently move into the same position.

The women talked and ate, Joanna complimenting Karin on the excellence of Suzette's cooking.

"Yes, I enrolled her in a cooking class. I deliberately selected one that had all women. I sent her to every evening class session wearing mascara and a little eyeliner, pantyhose and some rather feminine-style loafers. It wasn't long before they adopted her as their class sissy. But you enjoyed it didn't you?" Karin held out a morsel of food on the end of her fork.

"Yes, Mistress, the ladies in the class enjoyed me very much." Suzette leaned forward and gently took the food between her lips and pulled it off the fork.

"Such a good girl." Karin patted her sissy on the head.

Joanna followed likewise, offering Gary a piece of food which he rather clumsily ate from her fork. "Wow, feeding him like this is very erotic, makes me feel - powerful. Seeing them kneeling, so quiet, so submissive, and dependent on us for their food..."

Karin smiled, delighted that her Domme-in-training was readily taking to the indulgent way of life. "Yes, it's a little something I picked up from a friend. I felt the same way when I first watched her feed one of her 'babies' as she calls them. It's really the only way they should eat with us; otherwise they take their meals standing in the kitchen or from a dog dish on the floor."

They continued to eat and make small talk, the two sissies kneeling silently by their sides, being fed and stroked like beloved pets. Occasionally Suzette would rise and fill Karin's water glass, then immediately return to her submissive position. Gary followed, matching Suzette's every move and gesture, but without her fluid grace.

Nodding her head at Gary's copycat gestures Karin offered the explanation. "It's like animals in the wild, the young learn from watching and mimicking the actions of the older ones. Along with other behavioral modification techniques it makes a powerful transformation tool."

"So I can expect the same performance and service from Gary after he's completed the training?"

"I can almost guarantee it, assuming he doesn't have any actual learning disabilities." Karin reached down to stroke Suzette's cheek. "My little Suzette has helped me train many others haven't you?"

"Yes, Mistress."

"After the meal and when the girls have cleaned up, we'll take Gary downstairs and get him started. Would you like some dessert? I believe that Suzette has prepared something delicious."

"WHEN YOU'RE FINISHED PAINTING MY TOE NAILS STAY DOWN THERE AND BLOW ON THEM UNTIL THEY ARE DRY. BRENT LOVES THAT COLOR, SO I'LL WEAR THOSE CUTE PEEP-TOE PLATFORMS. WHEN MY TOES ARE DRY YOU CAN CRAWL TO MY CLOSET AND FETCH MY SHOES. MAKE SURE THEY ARE SHINED. IT'S SO NICE TO HAVE A SISSY CUCKOLD TO HELP ME GET READY FOR MY DATES. AREN'T YOU THE LUCKIEST HUSBAND EVER?"

Six

"*What's going to happen?*" asked Gary as he and Suzette put away the dishes.

"That's up to Mistress."

Gary was frustrated with, and envious of, Suzette. He was jealous of how accomplished she was in her movements and actions, how she always knew what to do. But it frustrated him that he couldn't get any real answers or information, other than domestic hints, from her. *Her, I'm thinking of her, him, as her. Shit! I could leave; walk out, right now, no one's stopping me.* "They talked about training me. What's that like?"

Suzette turned, cocked her head and stared at him. "It's training, we need it. It makes us better for Mistress."

Gary sighed and dropped his shoulders in surrender. *Mistress Karin is the real thing, a genuine dominant woman and I've never seen Joanna so sexy and powerful. I can go with this for a while longer, see where it leads.* "Are you like this all the time Suzette? I mean, are you always her servant, her slave? Do you always dress like this?"

Again, Suzette turned to him, her face blank, almost doll like. "These are the clothes I wear. I serve and obey Mistress. It's what I do. It's what you will do." In the recesses of her mind Suzette heard the sing-song voice: *It's fun to dress pretty. I like to wear makeup. I must obey Mistress.*

When the last dish was put away and the counter wiped clean Suzette took Gary's hand. "Come on, it's almost your time, I'll hold your leash."

Gary looked at her. He was frozen, unable to move.

"You need to crawl this time, on your hands and knees, behind me. I'll walk slowly; you can watch my high heels. I know you've been looking at them all day."

Gary felt the flush of crimson flood his cheeks. He *had* been watching her high heels all day. It started out first at his amazement that she could walk so easily in them. Eventually he forgot that Suzette was really a man and he got a thrill from watching the sexy maid mince about all day in the stilettos. The tug on his leash and collar jerked him to back reality. Unable to look Suzette in the face he dropped to his hands and knees.

Suzette reached down and patted him on the head. "Just be quiet and do what you're told." With a slight tug on the leash Suzette led them into the hallway.

Gary crawled behind, watching the light glint from the shiny black stilettos before him. *It's only a weekend. I can get through anything for a few days. Then we'll be home, back to normal.* Naked, on his hands and knees, Gary allowed the feminized male maid to lead him down the hallway and into the library where Karin and Joanna waited.

In Karin's richly appointed library she and Joanna relaxed with cigarettes and Cognac. The flickering light from candles cast warm shadows against the dark paneled wainscoting and the velvet drapes. Comfortably ensconced in rich leather chairs, the ladies awaited their submissive charges.

"He's adapted well it seems, no outbursts, no fighting back. He's obviously confused and clumsy in the execution of his duties, but those are things we can train into him." Karin flicked the ash from her cigarette and took a sip of her Cognac.

"I told you he likes to be dominated. And even though we've done the tying up and spanking thing, he's never met someone like you, someone who puts it all out there, who makes it real. I can sense that he's frightened, but there's no denying that he's been sporting an almost constant hard-on since we got here."

Karin laughed and nodded in agreement. "Exactly, our poor little Suzette has undoubtedly been cleaning up drools of pre-cum all afternoon and evening, not that she doesn't mind getting her hands on man spunk. But that erection is something we'll soon get under control. There's seldom a need for a sissy to be erect, unless we want to humiliate the poor thing. Ah, here comes our sissy-maid-to-be now."

The silk Persian rug on the library floor was a relief to Gary's hands and knees. He caught the scent of tobacco and perfume the minute he entered the room. Suzette led him to his Mistress, and with a delicate curtsey handed her the leash. Joanna accepted the proffered leash and Suzette backed away to kneel by Karin's chair.

Gary watched the flickering candlelight play over the gleaming patent leather of Joanna's high heeled pumps. She extended one of the wicked shoes and he leaned forward to reverently place a kiss on the toe.

Karin nodded her approval and reached over to pinch one of Suzette's nipples, causing the sissy maid to gasp. She mauled Suzette's nipples as her sissy moaned with pleasure. "Take Joanna's sissy to the basement and wait for us."

Karin and Joanna descended the basement steps and found Gary kneeling at the bottom, Suzette standing alongside, holding his leash. Karin took the leash from Suzette and pulled Gary along on his hands and knees. "Your training begins tonight. I expect you to do what you're told, total compliance. There will be no tolerance for disobedience."

Gary scampered along on his hands and knees as Karin pulled him into the room with the Breaking Cage. She guided Gary to the cage and allowed him a few moments to ponder his fate. "It's your new home for awhile. Here is where we begin your training."

His transformation began as Karin inserted the earphones into his ears. She affixed a CB-3000 chastity device. "This is not about you having any pleasure from that!" she added derisively. Next she attached the metal band and wire to his scrotum.

Confused and frightened, Gary sought out Joanna. She offered no consolation, but sat impassively smoking and met his gaze with cold, dead eyes.

Karin pulled his hands behind him and loosely laced him into an arm binder. "Not too tight, we don't want to interfere with his circulation, only restrict his movement and freedom."

Karin pulled the leather hood over Gary's head, padding the earpieces with cotton so the ear buds would seal and eliminate any outside noise. "A bit of sensory deprivation, for the next few days we will control everything he hears." Karin unsnapped the hood's eye piece so Gary could see. She walked to the end of the cage, opened the door and, with a flourish, beckoned Gary to crawl in.

In a panic Gary turned to Joanna who looked annoyed. "Go! Get in the fucking cage!"

Karin pushed a frightened Gary into the cage. She laughed as his knees hit the plastic spikes on the floor and he flinched. She kicked him with her pointed-toe pump, forcing him completely in. "Comfy?" she teased.

Karin shifted Gary within the cage, positioning him so he faced the nipple and face access doors. She pulled the wire attached to his scrotum ring and the wire to his earphone buds through the cage and hooked them to the control panel. She laughed at his frightened expression. "What, you thought it would be Joanna and I dressed in leather corsets and thigh-high boots? Some other time darling, first you need training and we're going to take care of that right now." She chuckled as Gary shifted his weight in the cage seeking relief from the tortuous plastic spikes, *and he hasn't even been in there but a few minutes! How is he going to feel tomorrow?* Karin picked up the microphone and switched it on, watching Gary jump at the sound. "Let me explain how this is going to work. You are going to be kept in the cage, locked in, for as long as we want to keep you there. You will hear recorded statements from time to time. You must repeat these statements, EXACTLY, within five seconds or you will be punished." Karin pushed a button on her console and Gary screamed in pain at the electrical current coursing through his scrotum. "Yes, that's what happens if you don't repeat what you hear."

"Please Joanna," Gary pleaded, "please we need to - aaaggghhh!"

Karin shocked him a second time and again Gary shrieked and twisted his body, seeking escape from the torment. Karin laughed and waved a finger back and forth, "Naughty, naughty, unauthorized talking is NOT allowed."

Gary slumped forward, defeated, quietly sobbing. Karin's voice sounded in his head. "Listen and repeat, or be punished. You will be given food and drink at regular intervals. Do NOT refuse this and consume ALL you are given."

Gary meekly nodded.

"Oh, our guest has arrived," Karin said.

Gary looked up through tear-stained eyes to see a tall and very handsome man walk in the room, extend a hand and help Joanna from her seat. He heard Karin's voice. "Of course you can't expect Joanna to sit idly by while you are trained to be a suitable slave, can you? Brent will see to her needs, make sure she isn't lonely for a real man."

Gary watched as Brent moved behind Joanna and pulled her into his arms. He recoiled as Brent leaned down to nuzzle Joanna's neck and Joanna melted into his embrace. When Brent moved his hand over Joanna's breast her head rolled back and she gasped in pleasure.

Tears streaked down Gary's face as he cried "No, please," and immediately received a shock for his vocal outburst.

Karin snapped his blindfold in place and the last thing Gary saw was Joanna waving to him, and mouthing the words 'bye-bye.'

Seven

Joanna picked up the remote from the bedside table. Brent lay naked beside her, the sheet barely covering him. She lifted the sheet and took a peek, *that is one magnificent cock!*

Only a few hours earlier she'd enjoyed her first extra-marital fuck since she'd married Gary. They'd left Gary to his cage experience and returned to Karin's library where Suzette served drinks and Joanna learned more about Brent. He was a corporate trainer and media consultant. At a commanding six-foot five, and with his good looks and rugged physique, Joanna could well imagine him dominating a room. He radiated power and authority, yet exhibited grace and charm with her, immediately putting her at ease.

In the basement, when she first laid eyes on

him, she knew she would give herself to him. Indeed, there was no hesitation to his first touch, when his lips met her neck it was electric. She'd easily yielded to his hand on her breast, because she wanted it there, and also because of the look on Gary's face. She was giving herself to another man, because she could, she had the power, she had the right. It was all part of the training, only she imagined she was going to enjoy her training much more than Gary.

The three of them enjoyed drinks and small talk until it was time to retire for the evening. Brent offered his arm and escorted Joanna to their bedroom. Even in her highest heels Joanna had to look up at Brent, something that was certainly not the case with Gary, *the Alpha male, once I've had that, how can I ever go back?*

Suzette was waiting in their bedroom. She'd turned down the bed and laid out their bedclothes, sexual toys and lotions and stood demurely to the side.

"It seems this is not your first time," Joanna said. "Do all the ladies get this kind of personal treatment?"

"I do what I can," he said, and gave a courtly bow.

Joanna laughed. "Hey, I'm not complaining. I've got it far better than my husband."

"Yes, you've each chosen your path. Consider me your guide and tutor. There are things I can help you with that are better left to me than with Karin."

Joanna licked her lips and took her gown from the bed. The gown was long, sheer black lace with Marabou trim and she pulled it seductively over her arm, loosely wrapping it around her as if she were being embraced by a python. "Let me slip into something more comfortable and the tutoring can begin."

Brent smiled as he watched her slink away. *I love my work.* He snapped his fingers and Suzette moved to attend him, helping him undress and bringing him a short, red silk robe.

Joanna's entrance from the bathroom had all the allure of old Hollywood. The black robe did little to hide the curves of her body, exactly her intent. Her hair was loose, framing her face with a sensuous auburn mane. She slinked across the floor, her stilettos now replaced with high heeled bedroom slippers trimmed in the same Marabou as the gown.

Brent caught the scent of her before she reached him. He reached out and tugged on the tie of her robe, allowing it to fall open. "I approve."

"I'm so glad," Joanna said. Her beautifully manicured fingers pulled apart the folds of his robe. When she looked down she literally gasped. "And I very much approve."

Brent snapped his fingers and Suzette appeared at their side, dropped to her knees and wiggled between them. Joanna watched as Suzette first kissed, then licked and finally took Brent's cock in her mouth.

Brent pulled Joanna into his arms. "She's a

fluffer, a living sexual aid," he said, nodding at Suzette. "She'll also clean up afterwards if we want."

Joanna felt Suzette trapped between them, felt the heat from Suzette's body, and watched the sissy maid's head bob up and down on that magnificent cock. Brent's lips kissed her neck as her arms snaked around him, her fingers teasing his muscular back. Brent's tongue gently traced a line around her ear and she shook from the sensation.

Through it all, Suzette continued to deep throat the cock.

"We'll train your husband to do that."

"Oh, god!" Joanna went weak in the knees, now totally supported in Brent's arms.

"Your husband, your maid, on his knees, getting a cock wet and hard for your pleasure."

She shook, wrapped her arms around him and pulled his lips down on hers. When his tongue found hers it was electric; she gave herself to him. Joanna ground her sex against Suzette's head, driving the sissy maid's face into Brent's crotch.

Brent broke the kiss and held her face in his hands. "It won't be long before you –"

"You talk too much. Do you fuck as well?"

He smiled and pulled her head to his chest. A quick snap of the fingers dismissed Suzette for the night. Brent swept Joanna into his arms and carried her across the room.

Joanna was surprised; no one had ever taken

her in such a manner. She nestled her head against his chest, kicked off her slippers and allowed herself to be carried to the bed of an Alpha Male.

That night Joanna learned she could enjoy pleasure with other men, that sissy maids were invaluable in preparing lovers, and that Alpha Males had a definite place in the hierarchy.

Following Karin's directions she punched in '91' on the TV remote and was rewarded with a video feed of Gary in the cage. She watched in silence until Gary said "I like to dress sexy for men." More silence followed and Gary said, "I like to suck cock. I like to wear mascara." Joanna smiled and shut off the TV. She slid under the covers and snuggled up to Brent, *yes, this is all going to work out just fine.*

"HOW IS SHE DOING, SWEETHEART? SHOWING YOU A GOOD TIME?"

"OH YEAH, YOU'VE TRAINED HER WELL, SHE HAS A MOUTH LIKE VELVET, SUCKS A GOOD COCK."

"WELL, I'M GLAD THAT WE'VE FOUND SOMETHING SHE'S GOOD AT BESIDES HOUSEWORK. KEEP SUCKING, SISSY. DOES IT TASTE GOOD?"

Eight

Brent and Joanna showered together, Joanna once more feeling the massive cock impaling her as Brent's strong hands caressed her breasts. She moaned as his thrust nearly lifted her off her feet. "So, do you do this for all of Karin's friends?"

He ran his hands down the side of her soapy body, cupping her bottom and pulling her further onto his shaft. "Some, not all, but yes, I've been known to help wives discover what they've been missing. The look on your husband's face last night, I've seen that before. It's a mixture of hurt, grief, despair, but ultimately acceptance. You're a free woman Joanna, your sexual fulfillment is just beginning." His mouth came down on hers as he lifted her up and felt her wrap her legs around him.

When the two came down for breakfast they found Karin, drinking coffee and reading the paper in the dining room. "Sleep well?"

Joanna returned a dazzling smile to both Karin and Brent. "Not that much actually, but it was one hell of a night."

"Most excellent darling, you've embarked on your own training regimen as well, although undoubtedly much more pleasant that that of your poor husband. Suzette will be serving breakfast shortly and then we'll give Gary his feeding."

Brent pulled out Joanna's chair and bent to give her a kiss when she was fully seated. He poured the both of them coffee. "And your newest project, it bodes well?"

Karin nodded and lit a cigarette. "Oh yes, I had Suzette run the printouts from last night. There was some resistance at first, he received a few initial shocks, but the performance log indicates that he quickly fell into the rhythm of the conditioned responses." She turned to Joanna, "Really, based on this preliminary data I don't expect any problems. By the end of the weekend you will be taking home a conditioned sissy. It was his nature; we're just reinforcing that and helping him come to grips with who and what he really is."

Suzette pushed a serving cart into the room and stopped to curtsey.

Karin crushed out her cigarette. "You may serve."

Suzette served the ladies first, offering plates of scrambled eggs and sausage. As she served Brent he ran his hand under her frilly maid's dress and fondled her balls. "Good morning Suzette."

Even with a hand groping her balls and while holding a serving tray, Suzette managed to effectively bob a curtsey. "Good morning Master."

Karin looked at Joanna and nodded to Brent and Suzette. "He teases and torments her so, but she loves the attention."

Joanna paused while eating. "Does he, I mean, do they…"

Karin smiled. "Does he fuck her? My god yes, you've had that marvelous cock, can you imagine how she squeals when he splits her with it?"

"So…would," Joanna searched for the words. "When Gary is trained, will he…"

Karin gestured and Suzette quickly moved to pour more coffee. Karin added sugar and stirred, "Joanna, Gary, or whatever you name 'her' will be whatever you want her to be. I prefer not to think of them as male or female, straight or gay; they're sissies, domestic maids who serve us. Their sexual life will be what we say it is: chastity, or servicing men, women, or other sissies. So to answer your question, yes, it's entirely conceivable that Brent may want to take Gary. He's had many of the girls I've trained, haven't you dear?"

Brent's eyebrows arched in a gleeful expression. "It's been my distinct pleasure to 'break in' some of these converts to sissydom." He reached over and pulled Suzette onto his lap and fondled her nipples. "The girls, after their initial anxiety, come to like it, don't you, baby?"

Suzette squirmed on his lap and licked her lips, "Oh yes, Master."

He threw her off, slapped her bottom and pushed her to the floor. "Get some bacon, you little trollop!" He laughed as she crawled to Karin.

Karin held out a piece of bacon and Suzette gently took it in her mouth. "Imagine your Gary sitting on an Alpha Male's lap, desperately wanting that male to play with his nipples." Karin put a bit of jam on a piece of toast and held it out for Suzette. "Or sliding under the table to take your date's cock in her mouth while you two enjoy a romantic dinner."

Joanna shook her head. "It's a lot to comprehend, way more than the bondage and spanking things we were doing." She quickly held up a hand. "Mind you, I'm NOT complaining." She smiled at Brent. "Not after last night."

"You'll both have to adjust," counseled Karin, "and you'll both be happier for it."

They gathered around the Breaking Cage as if they'd come to pay tribute to a holy shrine, to witness a sacrifice. Suzette held a silver tray containing two glass beakers, one with water, and one containing a thick gruel, an offering of sorts to their sacrificial victim. Joanna leaned into Brent, his arm wrapped around her.

The high priestess of the group, Karin, went to the computer console, disengaged the shock feature and turned down the white noise. Gary looked up as the irritating sound in his head vanished. Hooded, he couldn't see or hear, but he knew something in his limited, hellish environment had changed. She picked up the microphone and clicked it on. "Gary, I've turned off the shock feature but can use it at any time. Listen to my voice and follow my directions. Nod your head if you understand."

Gary slowly nodded his head and Karin turned off the microphone and smiled at the others. "He doesn't know what's happening; he's tired and confused, uncomfortable. Today and tomorrow the real conditioning begins, we've broken his initial resistance; he should now be much more receptive."

She turned the microphone back on. "Gary, we're going to feed you now. Do exactly as I say; move forward, to the side of the cage."

On legs and knees continually tormented by the tiny plastic spikes Gary crawled to the side of the cage until his face and body were pressed against the wire.

"Very good," purred Karin. "Suzette is going to feed you. You will open your mouth and suck the food from the feeding device. Nod if you understand."

Gary nodded.

Suzette poured the gruel into the eight inch dildo and screwed on the end cap. She opened the access door in front of Gary's face.

"Open your mouth, Gary, and take the feeding

cock. You'll have to suck hard to get it all." Karin switched off the microphone. "We'll give him a few minutes to feed."

The large flesh-colored dildo was bigger than Gary was prepared to take and he strained to open his mouth wider. He recoiled at the monstrous phallic invader as Suzette slowly pushed it in. Karin expected this and her elegant finger hit the punishment button. Gary screamed as the electrical shock tore through his genitals. Karin picked up the microphone. "You will take your food and water through the cock. Start sucking!"

Gary whimpered, but accepted the cock. As he began to suck, Suzette opened the access doors and caressed his nipples. He jumped at the sensation but quickly relaxed, pushing his breasts into the cage wire, offering his body to the tender fingers that toyed with his sensitive buds.

Once again Karin clicked on the microphone, her voice taking on a honeyed and sensuous tone. "You like that. Mmmm, it feels good to suck a cock, it gives you pleasure. Keep sucking, cocks have to be emptied, you want all of that cock juice inside you. Suck hard, you need to take it deep in your mouth and suck hard."

Suzette twisted Gary's nipples as he writhed in a mix of pain and pleasure. In his head he heard Karin's voice again, "Suck the cock, it gives you pleasure; it feels good." In another ten minutes Gary drained the feeding dildo and Suzette removed it from his mouth.

"Very good," came the voice. "Now open for

another cock, this is the cock that made love to Mistress Joanna last night. It's a big cock, a real man's cock and you need to thank it for pleasuring your Mistress."

Brent approached the cage and Karin used the electric hoist to position the cage so Gary's mouth was at perfect cock-sucking level. Suzette knelt before Master Brent, unzipped his pants and pulled out his cock. She gave his cock a reverent kiss of respect and backed away.

"Kiss Master's cock, show it the respect it deserves," Karin said.

Brent slowly rubbed his cock over Gary's lips as Gary tried to kiss it.

Karin motioned to Joanna and held out the microphone. "He needs to hear your voice, to know it's you that wants him to suck the cock, to know that you've been pleasured by this cock."

Joanna took the microphone and felt Brent wrap his arm around her and pull her close. The two lovers watched as Brent continued to toy with Gary's mouth, teasing Gary's lips with his cock.

"Gary," Joanna softly said, watching him jump at the sound of her voice. "I want you to suck this beautiful cock for me, baby, take it in your mouth, feel it and taste it. It's a wonderful cock and I took my pleasure from it last night - and again this morning."

Gary was moaning but it was difficult for Joanna to tell if it was pleasure or disgust as Brent began to slowly inch his enormous cock into Gary's mouth. "That's it, baby, suck it. You're going to be my cocksucker from now on, you'll get them nice and hard for me and you'll lick them clean when I'm done with them. You will pleasure my lovers in this way, and I'll take my pleasure by watching you do it, on your knees, sucking cocks for me. Oh, I think he's gonna come and I can tell you baby, he comes a lot. Swallow it, taste my lover, get to know that taste."

Brent shot streams of sticky cum into Gary's mouth and Gary jerked back, strands of cum dripping down his mouth onto his chest.

Karin pushed the punishment button, Gary reeled in pain, and then she pressed it again. She took the microphone from Joanna and spoke menacingly, "When you suck you suck until the man is through with you, you lick and swallow as long as it pleases your Mistresses and Masters!"

Gary nodded and put his tear-streaked face back up to the cage. Brent offered his now deflated cock, placing it in Gary's waiting mouth as Gary sucked and licked it clean until Brent removed it.

"Better," Karin said. "Suzette will now give you some water, in a cock. Drink it all and then we will resume your training."

Sobbing with despair Gary opened his mouth, accepted the watering cock and began to suck it dry.

"And what," asked Joanna, "this cycle gets repeated?"

"Exactly, more or less," Karin said. "We may not do any more cock sucking, depends if we have suitable males available, but yes, the conditioning will go on like this for another night and day. We'll re-evaluate at that point, see where we are and what we need to do next. He hasn't even been in here for twelve hours yet."

"It looks like he's already breaking, I mean, he sucked a cock. He's never done that."

"I agree. I think we're making excellent progress." Karin watched Suzette remove the watering cock and close up the access panels in the side of the cage. Turning to the computer console Karin started the white noise droning into Gary's earphones and engaged the random recitation program. "Would everyone like a Mimosa?"

"Sure," replied Joanna, as she took Brent's hand.

As they ascended the stairs the silence was broken by Gary's voice. "I like to wear high heels. I'm a fuck toy. It's good for Mistress to have lovers."

"IT'S NICE, BUT I WAS REALLY LOOKING FOR SOMETHING MORE DOMESTIC. DO YOU HAVE ANYTHING IN A TRADITIONAL MAID'S DRESS?"

"YOU HAVE A MAID?"

"ACTUALLY IT'S FOR MY HUSBAND. HE'S MEETING MY LOVER THIS WEEKEND AND I WANT HIM TO LOOK PRETTY."

"OH! YOU HAVE A SISSY MAID? I'D REALLY LIKE ONE. MY SISTER HAS ONE AND IT'S SO CONVENIENT."

"I QUITE AGREE. I DON'T KNOW HOW I EVER GOT ALONG WITHOUT ONE. ABOUT THE DRESS?"

"OH YES, I HAVE JUST THE THING. AND HE'LL NEED A PETTICOAT AND STOCKINGS, TOO."

Nine

Life was different for Joanna and Gary. A new world of Female Domination had opened for Joanna and she was embracing it, living it to the fullest.

On Sunday afternoon they removed a quiet and shaken Gary from the Breaking Cage. Karin instructed Suzette to put Gary in a warm bath and give him soup and a Brandy. While Suzette provided the necessary after-care, Karin and Joanna plotted the strategy for Gary's further subjugation.

"It's important that you reinforce the conditioning," Karin advised. "Don't let him backslide or fall into old habits. You don't have to be cruel or vicious; there'll be time enough for that kind of play later. But be consistent, firm and unyielding. He's a bit shell-shocked right now, and as some of that wears off there may be some confusion for him. You must become that rock of feminine authority that anchors him in his place."

"I think I can do that, I've been watching how you interact with Suzette, it all seems so natural," Joanna said.

"Yes, well, Suzette is obviously at a more advanced state of training, but yes, there is something in what you say. Adopt that uncompromising and demanding dominant female voice and Gary will fall in line. It's his nature; we've only brought it to the fore and given him permission to be who he is. Brent's seen this all before, haven't you, darling."

Brent took a final drink of his Scotch and placed the empty tumbler on the table. "As Karin says, it's who he is; you wonderful ladies are simply allowing a man to let the sissy inside flower to full bloom."

"Are you inferring he's a pansy?" mocked Joanna, and they all laughed at the pun.

"We know what you mean," Karin said as she watched Brent rise to his feet. "Are you leaving dear?"

"Yes, my work here, for the moment, is finished." He walked to Joanna, pulling her from her chair and into his arms. "Although I'd like to continue to provide any services or counseling you may require." His mouth came down on hers in a long and intimate kiss.

When they broke the kiss Joanna brushed a strand of hair from her face and took a deep breath. "Yes, I'd like that. I'd like that very much."

"Give it a week or two and then you can formally introduce Gary to his new Master. By then both of you will have started to institutionalize your roles and habits. Of course," laughed Karin, "that doesn't mean that Mistress Joanna and Master Brent can't get together as often as needed in the interim to - consult."

"I'll call you then," smiled Brent as he gave Joanna a final kiss and took his leave.

Karin and Joanna lingered over their coffee as they waited for Suzette to bring Gary to them.

When Suzette arrived she led Gary by a leash attached to his collar. Gary was naked, save for a black skirt. He plodded along, his bare feet slapping on the tile floor accompanied by the clicks of Suzette's stilettos. Suzette stopped before Joanna, curtsied and offered the leash in her hand.

Joanna nodded approvingly and took the leash. With a tug on the leash Joanna pulled Gary to her side. Joanna dropped the leash on the floor and commanded Gary to, "Crawl to Karin, kiss her feet and thank her for having us this weekend."

Without hesitation Gary dropped to his knees and crawled to Karin, halting before her gleaming black patent high heels and bending forward to plant kisses on her toes. "Thank you Mistress, for having Mistress Joanna and I to your house." As Karin nonchalantly lifted her shoe, Gary lovingly licked the sole.

Joanna and Karin shared a knowing smile.

The ride home was subdued. Joanna drove, while Gary sat quietly, clad in only the skirt and collar. "You're off work tomorrow so I'll allow you some time to rest from the weekend's ordeal," Joanna explained. "But I do have some things you need to get done."

"Yes, Mistress."

"Tomorrow you will move all of your things out of my bedroom and into the small room at the end of the hall; we'll call it the maid's room."

"Yes, Mistress."

"I'll explain more of the new rules as we go along. You haven't changed your mind?"

"Oh no, Mistress."

"Good, I'm going to give you all the domination you've ever craved." *And we've already changed your mind.*

At home Joanna took the leash and led Gary to her bedroom as Gary followed meekly behind carrying Joanna's bags. "Take off that skirt, unpack my bags and put my things away. I'm going to relax."

Without thinking, Gary's fingers grasped the hem of his skirt and he bobbed a clumsy curtsey to acknowledge Joanna's orders. She relaxed in her chair and watched him unpack her bag. When he finished she extended a foot. "Put lotion on my feet."

Gary reached for the bottle of lotion and knelt before her; squirting a pool of lotion into his palm he began to lovingly work the silky cream in Joanna's foot.

Joanna lit a cigarette, closed her eyes and enjoyed the ministrations of her now devoted slave/husband. *Oh yes, I can definitely get used to this, a loving and slavishly devoted husband to see to my every need and a well-hung stud like Brent in my bed. Karin, you are a gift to women everywhere.* "On my legs as well, I want them soft and silky for Brent."

When she was satisfied with her legs she stood and turned, "A little on my bottom," and soon felt Gary's hands caressing her pert derriere. She laughed and wiggled. "Give it a little kiss and we can go to bed."

Joanna gathered up his leash in her hand and pulled him towards the bed. At the foot of the bed she looped his leash around the bedpost. He remained, silent, on his knees, waiting the bidding of his Mistress.

She threw a pillow and blanket on the floor. "You'll sleep here tonight. Tomorrow we will arrange for your new accommodations."

"Yes, Mistress."

Joanna stood before him and extended a foot, smiling when he bent forward to place a kiss on it. "Goodnight, sleep tight," she mocked.

"Goodnight, Mistress."

As she luxuriated under the covers she heard Gary settling in on the floor. But her thoughts, as she drifted into slumber, weren't about the submissive tethered to the end of her bed; she dreamt of Brent and that lovely cock that pleasured her so.

The next morning Joanna arose to find Gary huddled in a fetal position, wrapped in a blanket at the foot of her bed. At some point during the night he'd managed to finally drift off to sleep on the hard and unforgiving floor. *Time to get up my little slut, there's more training to do.* She took the leash from the bedpost and gave it a tug, watching him awake in a daze. "Up, I need coffee. Go make it now, wait, first we need this." Joanna took a penis gag from her bedside drawer and forced it into his mouth, tightly cinching the buckle in the back. Gary heard the ominous 'click' of a lock. "Until you're properly trained to eat and drink only when and what I tell you, I need to make sure you don't sneak anything behind my back, understand?"

Gagged, Gary simply nodded and give a half-hearted curtsey.

Joanna unclipped the leash from his collar, turned him around and gave him a swat on his ass to send him on his way, "Coffee, now!" As her new sissy maid toddled off to make coffee, Joanna fell into the bed, languorously sliding the covers up around her. *A spoiled and pampered bitch, that's what I'm going to become.* She took a pen and notepad from her nightstand and made notes: *Sell his truck, New car for me, Re-paint the maid's room, Ear piercing, Salon appointment, Daily exercise and diet, Finances.*

Before Gary returned with the coffee she finished her notes and placed the paper in the drawer. *No sense scaring him all it once, but by the end of the week things will be very different around here.* When he entered the room Joanna gave an appreciative nod to the coffee service on the silver tray. "Very nice, it pleases me when you perform this well. Does it please you as well?"

Gary enthusiastically shook his head 'Yes.'

"Then you like being a sissy maid?"

She smiled at the affirmative bob of his head and pointed to the floor at the side of her bed, "Kneel here and we'll have a little talk. Well, I'll talk and you simply nod yes or no, understand?"

'Yes.'

"Do you like it when I dominate you, when I dress sexy, when I tease and torment you?"

'Yes.'

"Did you think Karin was sexy? Did you like being dominated by her?"

'Yes.'

"You like to submit to women; you want more of that don't you?"

'Yes.'

"Do you want to be a pretty sissy maid like Suzette?" He hesitated and she took his nipple in her fingers and toyed with it, watching him sigh and quiver. She smiled when he slowly nodded, 'Yes.'

"You want to have your cock locked away and wear pretty clothes?"

'Yes.'

"But I still need a cock to make me happy." She pinched and twisted the nipple, loving the way he moaned through the gag. "I'm still going to need a real cock to fill me and give me pleasure; don't you agree?" Her nipple torment continued.

He closed his eyes and nodded, 'Yes.'

"So you're going to be my pretty sissy maid slave and do whatever I want, wait on me hand and foot, obey my every whim."

'Yes, yes.'

"And I'll lock your little cock away, let's call it a clitty from now on, and I'll control your sexual releases. But I'll still have all the lovers and cocks I want - OK?" Her finger nails cut into his nipple and she felt him shake with, *what - pain, pleasure?* "OK, lots of sex for me and almost none for you, OK?"

'Yes, yes, yes.'

"Stand up! Look at your little clitty, it's trying to get hard like a real man's would. We're certainly going to have to lock that up. Oh sweetheart, it's leaking, you've got some sissy cream. You must be excited about all the things we've discussed, aren't you." Using her fingernails she lightly stroked the length of his cock. As his knees buckled his shaft got harder. *We'll fix this!* She grasped his balls and squeezed. The pain made him want to drop to his knees but she held him fast and he writhed on the balls of his feet.

"I don't need this thing to get hard!" she spat. "It's fucking useless to me for sexual pleasure. The sooner we get it locked up and put away the better. Then you can concentrate on ME rather than this useless piece of crap between your legs. Are you a sissy maid?"

'YES, YES, YES,' he nodded

"And do sissy maids have cocks?"

'NO, NO, NO.'

"So we should lock this away?"

'YES, YES, YES.'

When she released her grip he calmed down and simply stood in place, shaking.

"Good, just as long as we understand one another. You're a sissy maid with a locked up clitty. I can have as many cocks as I want." She viciously slapped his cock and balls, "Agreed?"

'Yes, yes.'

"Clear away this coffee, I'm going to shower. If you want to jack off you better do it now. It may be a long time before you touch that thing again."

Gary gathered up the coffee tray and carried it downstairs to the kitchen. Not knowing exactly why, he quickly washed the items and put them away. *I must always keep a clean and tidy house for Mistress.* But Joanna's last words rang in his ears and as soon as he'd wiped down the counters he folded the wash cloth, put it away and immediately grabbed his cock. Pulling feverishly at himself he pummeled his manhood seeking that one last blessed relief. Although he became semi-rigid he wasn't achieving a full erection. Panic set it, *if I can't get hard I can't cum and if I don't do it now, then when...* He pulled harder and faster; frustration was overtaking him. When he heard the shower water turn off he reluctantly released his grip on his cock and rushed upstairs to grab a towel.

Joanna was impatient. "Next time be waiting

when I get out of the shower; on your knees, with a clean dry towel in your arms. Dry my legs."

Gary dropped to his knees, shuffled forward and dried Joanna's legs.

"Enough," she said, "up!"

As he rose to his feet she spun him around. Gary felt her handling the lock and the buckle on the dreaded penis gag and then she slid it out of his mouth. He stretched his jaws and breathed deeply. Before he could regain his composure she spun him around again so he was now facing her.

She held the evil gag before his eyes. "You mouth off, talk back, eat or drink when and what you're not supposed to and it goes back in - understand?"

"Yes, Mistress."

"As long as you do what you're told, when you're told to do it in exactly the way you're told to do it won't go so badly for you. I'm not saying it will be easy, but if you fuck up it will be much worse. Did you jack off?"

"Yes, Mistress."

"And did you cum?"

His head fell to his chest and he fought back tears. "No, Mistress."

She heard the regret and despair in his voice, "Not my problem, you had your chance. You'll have to earn the right to another and it won't be easy." She dropped her towel on the floor, walked to the toilet and sat down. "Crawl over here and kiss my feet while I pee, then you can lick me clean. And after that - we lock up your little clitty."

After Joanna dressed she was true to her word and marched Gary to the shower where she made him shave off all his body hair. "You're to keep yourself smooth and hairless at all times."

While Gary showered and removed his body hair Joanna prepared to install his chastity device. When he emerged from the shower she clamped a bag of ice to his cock, noting with glee how it shriveled at the frigid onslaught. With deft hands she lubricated his penis, fit the rings and spacers and slid the cage over his cock, securing it with a tamper-proof numbered tag. "There we go, all locked away. You'll learn to obtain sexual gratification in other ways. You'll learn that your pleasure comes from pleasing others."

"Yes, Mistress." In his head Gary heard the voice: *It's good to be a fuck toy.*

"YES, THAT'S MUCH BETTER. YOU LOOK VERY SWEET WITH YOUR SMOOTH SKIN AND CHASTITY DEVICE."

"NO, I DON'T KNOW WHEN YOU WILL BE LET OUT. AND DON'T ASK ME AGAIN OR IT WILL BE A VERY L-O-N-G TIME. NOW DOWN ON YOUR KNEES, THERE'S NO REASON FOR ME TO BE DENIED WHATEVER PLEASURE I WANT."

Ten

Over the next two weeks Joanna put her plans into action, her hastily scrawled notes charting the enslavement and submission of Gary. The same day she'd locked the chastity device on him she moved him out of her bedroom.

"The room down the hall, the small guest room, will be your new room," she told him. "It will be the maid's room. Move all of your things out of my room. I've ordered you a new bed and dresser to be delivered on Saturday. Before then you need to re-paint. These are the color samples."

In disbelief he took the color strips from her hand. The walls were to be done in a pastel pink with gloss ivory trim around the rest of the room, "Yes, Mistress."

"It's Bubblegum, the pink color," she chirped. "Don't you just love it?"

He nodded, barely whispering, "Yes, Mistress."

"I want you to do a good job, make the room nice and pretty. I'll certainly want to show it off to our friends." She handed him a large plastic bag, "These are your working clothes, for things like painting and house projects when you can't wear a maid's uniform."

"Thank you." He nervously opened the plastic bag and pulled out coveralls, or what used to be coveralls.

"Aren't these simply the cutest things? The Korean lady, the seamstress at the strip mall did it for me."

Gary held out the coveralls. They'd been dyed a bright pink and the legs had been cut off to a clam digger length and finished with purple lace. Likewise the sleeves had been removed and the arm holes again trimmed in the same purple lace. 'SISSY MAID' was embroidered across the back in bright purple and a red heart and a purple poodle appliqué adorned each breast pocket.

"There's more," Joanna laughed, clapping her hands.

As he reached into the bag he removed additional items: purple floral lace pantyhose, bright pink ladies work gloves, and large clip-on hoop earrings. At the bottom of the bag lay his 'work boots.'

"Try them on," Joanna said.

They did look somewhat like work boots, or at least a demented fashion designer's idea of what a fetish, sissy maid work boot would be. They were a brown suede, lace up with a pointed toe. The heel had to be almost five inches and while not a stiletto was still slender. They extended past his ankle and had padding at the top in the fashion of a typical work boot. Mumbling what he hoped was taken as appreciative thanks Gary put on the boots.

"No, I want to see the whole outfit, now!"

He bobbed a curtsey and stripped, ready to give his Mistress a fashion show. When he was dressed Joanna made him walk around the room, pose and simulate painting.

"Oh, that is *so* precious. I'm going to have to get some pictures and video of you working, getting your sissy maid room all ready. Tomorrow, on the way home from work you're to stop and get the paint. After you serve dinner and clean up tomorrow I want you up here and working on this room. It has to be done before the furniture comes on Saturday."

"Yes, Mistress."

"You may prepare supper now; call me when you're ready to serve. And keep the outfit on; I think it's cute."

Mid-week, as Gary was finishing the supper dishes he heard the ringing of the crystal bell. He quickly wiped his hands, straightened his apron and made his way to the living room. His ability to walk in high heels was improving. Joanna insisted he always wear them in the house and had started him out with a three inch heel, telling him that he would be expected to wear ever-increasingly higher heels. He stopped before Joanna and bobbed a curtsey.

Joanna noted with satisfaction that his ability to walk in heels and his curtseys were improving every day. And why not, when one wore high heels for hours every day and curtsied constantly. "I called your boss and scheduled you for a day off this Friday. I have some things planned. Are you finished in the kitchen?"

"I'm nearly done, Mistress."

"You can finish in there later. Do my feet."

Gary retrieved his pedicure basket from behind the sofa, and spread a towel on the floor beneath Joanna's feet. As she raised a leg he gently took her foot in hand and began to lovingly massage it.

Joanna relaxed and closed her eyes. This was an indulgence that she was easily becoming accustomed to.

After the foot massage Gary used a Swedish File to remove any rough spots and ended with yet another massage, this one with a moisturizing lotion. When he finished he gave her foot a reverent kiss and slowly lowered it to the floor. He took her other foot into his hand, gave it a kiss and then repeated the same process.

Through it all Joanna reveled in the loving attention rendered to her peds. *Mmmm, a husband/sissy maid to serve me and Brent's cock to fuck me, I am one lucky woman.*

The loving foot worship of the night before was quickly forgotten the next morning. "Slut, get your ass in here!" Joanna screamed.

A fearful Gary ran to the voice from Joanna's bathroom. He stopped at the door, executed a nervous curtsey and awaited his fate. Given the look on Joanna's face it didn't bode well.

"What the fuck is THAT?" Joanna pointed an elegantly manicured fingernail at the jagged edge on the toilet paper . "Have I not been explicit in my needs? Have I not trained you? Are you TRYING to piss me off?"

Unsure of what to say, Gary executed another curtsey which only angered Joanna.

"Don't fucking stand there and bob at me! Get your ass over here!"

As he approached she reached out and slapped him, hard, across the face. She grabbed him by the hair and jerked his head towards the toilet paper dispenser. "Look at that; do you see what's wrong?"

"It's, I mean the…"

She jerked up his head and slapped him again. "The fold, idiot, where's the cute little fold I taught you to put on the end of the toilet paper?"

"I – uh – I…"

She grabbed a nipple, squeezing it, pinching and twisting until the pain drove him to his knees, then she slapped him again. "Every time I pee or shit, in any bathroom in this house I expect to see the toilet paper end folded, exactly like I taught you. Is that too fucking much to ask?"

"No, Mistress."

"You've got me so upset that I made a mess," she pulled his face to the toilet seat where yellow drops of pee glistened. "Now, I want you to lick this clean, and for good measure, when you're done here, I want you to lick every toilet seat in this house spotlessly clean. And put that fold on all the toilet paper rolls! You're lucky I even use toilet paper any more. I could just as easily use your tongue and mouth for all my toilet needs and save myself the cost of toilet paper, couldn't I?"

"Yes, Mistress."

"Then do a better job in the future. Close your eyes and open your mouth."

Gary closed his eyes and opened his mouth, scared of what might follow, but fearing even worse consequences if he disobeyed.

Joanna took the piece of toilet paper from her pocket, the one she'd torn off before he entered, the piece perfectly folded into a triangle. She pushed the paper into his mouth. "Chew and swallow, and then you've got some toilet seats to clean."

On Friday morning, clad only in his heels and a small apron that covered nothing and revealed everything, Gary prepared and served breakfast. As he did the dishes Joanna reminded him of their appointment. "We're having a salon day; I've laid out your clothes on your bed. You did a very good job painting your room, and just in time too; your new furniture comes tomorrow. Do you like the color?"

"Oh yes, Mistress, very much." Actually the pink Bubblegum color was unnerving but he didn't have a choice.

"Go and change, we need to be there at ten."

When Gary got to his room he saw the clothing Joanna had selected for their outing: a pink lacy bra and panty set, women's black slacks that zipped up the side, a white woman's blouse, black lace trouser socks and black loafers that were definitely feminine in design. From a distance he might look male, but up close anyone discern a definite sissy look. The blouse was sheer enough to reveal the outline of the pink bra beneath. But Gary didn't balk and simply began to dress, the voice in his head somehow reassuring, *I like to wear pretty things.*

Joanna used the interlude to make a call to Karin. "Yes, it's going fine, no real resistance, only some hesitation now and then. Yes, I did the bathroom thing; it seemed to shock him a bit."

"But it's good to keep them off balance," advised Karin. "Mixing in the loving female authority and dominance with moments of terror and humiliation keep them finely honed in that submissive mode. When do you introduce him to Brent?"

"Soon, I think he's ready. Of course I've been seeing Brent, just not openly at the house. I think Gary knows that I'm seeing someone, but he simply accepts it."

"Is he still in chastity?"

"Oh yes, really no reason to have the little thing out and about is there?"

Karin laughed. "Not unless you feel like toying with it. Control the orgasm and control the man, or in this case, the sissy."

"Yes, I've learned that. We're going to the salon today; I've got a few surprises in store for him."

"Wonderful, call if you need anything."

They arrived at the salon a little before ten. Gary had been there before, but only to drop off or pick up Joanna; today he was a client. A slim thirtyish woman with spiky hair rushed forward to give Joanna an air kiss. "Hey, good to see you, and Gary is here for his very first beauty treatment?"

Gary nodded his head and gave a quiet, "Yes Ma'am."

"Ma'am!" the woman laughed, "my name is Marie and I'll be doing you today. Joanna, Claire is ready for you." Marie took Gary's hand. "Follow me back here sweetie and we'll get started."

As Marie took Gary's hand he turned to see Joanna give him a smile and a little wave.

Marie pulled him through a set of curtains and into a room with a door. "This is one of our private rooms, for special clients. Joanna is spoiling you," she teased. "Now, you have the option of sitting still and doing what you are told, or we can strap you down. Are you going to be a good girl?"

Her teasing voice and 'good girl' reference seemed to trigger something in Gary; *I will always be a good girl.* "I'll be good, Ma'am."

Marie smiled and patted him on the head. "I know sweetie, I've done your kind before. Just relax and enjoy it. Now take off all your clothes. You can hang them on that hook, and then put on this gown and get in the chair." She handed him a pink dressing gown.

Marie seated Gary in the chair and draped a cloth around his neck. "Joanna picked out some nice colors for you, are you excited?"

"Yes, Ma'am."

"Your hair is getting longer and Joanna wants you to keep growing it out, but we're giving it a few highlights today. When I'm finished with the highlights Becky will be in to work on you."

He watched in the mirror as Marie went to work, separating out strands of hair, coating them with a smelly goop and wrapping them in foil. Gary thought he looked ridiculous, but had no choice other to sit and endure. *A good sissy obeys.*

When she was done Marie turned the chair around so Gary could check out his new hairstyle. He was shocked to see his hair much lighter, almost blond, with reddish-bronze streaks.

"Wow, that looks really hot on you" Marie said.

"Yeah - uh, yes Ma'am - very - hot." *How can I go to work next week, how can I even walk out of here?*

True to her word, when Marie was done with the highlights she left the room and a few minutes later a plump, freckle-faced blonde no more than twenty entered the room. "Hi, I'm Becky. I've never done a sissy before, you'll be my first. Oops, sorry, is it OK to call you a sissy?" she giggled.

"Yes, Ma'am."

"Ma'am! You are so cute!" She pulled up a stool and sat down. "OK, first they wanted you cleaned up down here." As she talked she pulled open his gown exposing Gary's chastised member. "Wow! Is that like really locked up?"

"Yes, Ma'am."

She grabbed the device, moving it around and examining it. "Don't think I'd want to be locked up and not be able to come. Does it hurt?"

"No, Ma'am, I'm getting used to it."

"Whatever, anyway, I'm gonna clean up around it. Your wife says she wants it as smooth and hairless as I can get it." She reached over and flicked the switch on a small device. "While the wax heats up I'll do your eyebrows, OK?"

Gary leaned back and closed his eyes as Becky rolled her stool by his head and tilted back his chair. She chatted non-stop as she expertly tweezed his eyebrows. The process seemed to go on for so long that Gary began to wonder if he was going to have any eyebrows left.

Finally she was done and Gary felt his chair rise to a sitting position.

"OK, sissy, you can open your eyes," Becky said.

He opened his eyes to see Becky standing before him holding a mirror. "They look great, very sexy; you'll just need to touch them up with a bit of eyebrow pencil. I'll show you how to do that and give you one in your shade before you leave today."

He blinked his eyes to focus and gazed into the mirror. His eyebrows were now very thin and arched. For a moment a wave of panic set in, *how can I go to work like this? I look like...*But the voice reassured him, *I like to look sexy for men.* For a moment he was silent, then he said, "Very nice, thank you very much."

"Cool!" She checked her can of wax. "OK, now we can do the wax. They said that if you made noise during the waxing I was s'posed to gag you. You gonna be a quiet sissy?"

"I'll try, Ma'am."

"OK." She gathered her wax and cloth strips and went to work. The warm wax felt nice, but when she ripped the first one off he yelped. "OK, you're s'posed to be quiet. One more cry and I'm gonna gag you like they said."

Gary nodded. It hurt like hell and he cried out as she pulled off the second strip.

Becky stood. "OK, I gave you two chances."

He watched as her hands disappeared under her dress and she wiggled out of her panties. She held them over his face and smiled, "Open up."

Gary opened as she carefully inserted her panties, the moist crotch first, into his waiting mouth. Then she reached into a drawer and removed a long strap, drawing it around his mouth and the chair, using it to secure his head and hold the panty gag in place. "OK, let's finish this up; I need to go on break." She efficiently waxed his crotch smooth and hairless, often turning to flash him an evil smile as he groaned into her panty gag.

"Almost done," she chortled. "Now lift your legs up - way up."

She lifted his legs and applied the wax and cloth strips to the hairs on his ass. Tears streaked down his face when she pulled them off. "OK sissy, I'm through here for now. I'll be back for more beauty stuff later. You can keep the panties."

He was left alone for several minutes before Marie breezed back into the room. She threw back his dressing gown and ran her hands over his crotch. "Very nice, Becky does a lovely job." She smiled as she looked at his gag. "You were a naughty sissy weren't you? Do her panties taste nice?"

Gary nodded in the affirmative.

"Let's just leave them in a while longer shall we? Joanna is finished, she and a gentleman left for a romantic lunch. She'll be back later in the afternoon for you. But in the meantime we've lots more work to do on you. It will be about twenty minutes before your next treatment. I'm gonna close the door and turn out the lights. You just sit there and nap like a good sissy."

Alone, in the dark, Gary tried to make sense of everything. His hair was streaked blond and red, his crotch and ass were hairless and his eyebrows were thin and arched. And Joanna was out on a date, a romantic luncheon date. She'd been out a lot lately; getting all dressed up, going out to dinner, leaving him home alone with a long list of chores to insure he stayed busy. She never said what she was doing, or where she was going, and he knew it wasn't his place to ask. *Of course I'm locked up, Mistress doesn't need a sissy clitty, but she still needs a cock.*

He dozed off and was startled when the door opened and the lights came on. Becky smiled at him as she pushed a cart into the room. "Hey sissy, have a nice nappy? See you still have my panties." She undid the strap and pulled the panties out of his mouth. "Ick, you can keep these, I don't want them now." She put them in a zip-loc bag and set them on a chair, "A little souvenir of your visit. I'm gonna do your nails now, toenails and fingernails. Joanna wants you to have bright red toenails, but she is willing to start you off with just a pale pink fingernail polish, OK?"

"Yes, Ma'am."

"I like your hair, it's way cute."

Gary simply nodded.

She set to work on his feet first, telling him that Joanna was going to expect him to do this for himself in the future so he needed to pay attention to what she was doing and how. When she was done Gary looked down to see ten glossy red toenails gleaming in the light.

"Pretty," remarked Becky.

"Yeah." *I want to wear sexy high heels to show off my pretty feet.*

Before moving up to work on his fingernails Becky pulled back the gown to look at his crotch. "Oh yeah, much better," she ran her hand over the skin, "s-m-o-o-t-h."

She left the gown open, exposing the chastity device and went to work on his nails, again advising him to pay attention so he could do his own nail care. When she finished she stood, "OK, we'll let these dry and then do your ears." Without another word she got up and pushed her cart out the door, leaving it open behind her. His dressing gown was still open exposing himself, but he hadn't received permission to close it.

For the next ten minutes a parade of women

came in and out of the room, silently observing him and looking at his chastity device. They came singly and in pairs. Gary couldn't believe they were all staff or employees; was he being put on display for the customers? The women looked at his hair, eyebrows and nails, but most were intrigued by the chastity device. They lifted it up, turned it, gave it a slight tug to test its security and used their fingernails to poke at his cock through the ventilation slits. While many made remarks or comments none were directed at him, so Gary remained mute during the humiliating display and inspection process: "I wonder why they let themselves be treated like this...I must get one of these for my husband...It must be terribly frustrating...How cute, I love the pink color...She says he serves as her maid...Well I can see why she had the luncheon date today...I wonder if she'd rent him out to clean?"

Becky returned when the parade of curious onlookers stopped. "OK ,sissy, you're gonna get your ears pierced." She glanced down to see his exposed, chastity-enclosed cock, "Been exposing yourself you bad boy?" she teased. She slapped it with her hand and giggled, "Bad sissy, bad sissy."

Gary closed his eyes at the shame of it and felt her throw the dressing gown back over him.

"I was hoping I'd get to pierce your tongue, it would make you WAY better at eating pussy, but Marie said not this time. Joanna only wants your ears pierced. I'm trying to talk her into getting a ring in your nose, put a little chain on it and I guarantee you'd follow her anywhere." At that she giggled again and tweaked his nose. "But Joanna got you these swell studs, they're really nice, she must like you a lot."

He watched her fiddle with some kind of machine and then felt her grab his ear.

"It's just a little prick, oh, I made a joke! Girls get this done all the time." She paused, "I guess sissies, too!" and giggled again.

Within minutes she was cleaning up and putting her tools away. When she finished she turned Gary to look in the mirror.

The reflection was not one he immediately recognized. His hair was blond with red streaks, his eyebrows thin and arched and now his ears were pierced. When he put his hands up to touch his ears he saw the perfectly manicured pink nails.

"Almost done, Diane will be in to finish you up."

He gave Becky a quizzical look as if to ask what more could be done to him, "Diane?"

"The cosmetician, it was fun, I hope you come back. I like doing sissies." With a little pat-pat of her hand on his chastity device Becky smiled and strode out the door.

Two hours later Joanna returned to claim Gary. In the interim Diane had given him a full makeover: foundation, lips, false eyelashes, eye makeup. To pass the time waiting for Joanna, Marie gave him a simple black smock and made him serve tea and coffee to her customers. Everyone seemed quite taken with the new help, both in his appearance and his servile manner.

Joanna thanked Marie and settled the bill for the day's work. She hardly paid any attention to Gary who continued to scoot about the salon, filling coffee and fetching magazines.

Finally she turned to Gary, "Come dear, we need to leave. Pick up your clothes; they're in the bag there."

Obediently, Gary picked up the plastic bag containing the clothes he'd worn in and meekly followed Joanna outside and to the car. No one seemed to notice the strange looking creature with the streaked hair and dressed in the black smock.

Joanna slid into the front seat and lit a cigarette. "Did you enjoy your day of pampering?"

"Yes, Mistress, very much, thank you."

"Good, it can be a reward for excellent behavior. Becky wanted me to give you a nose ring." She watched him wince at the thought. "I might consider it and your nipples as well. Are you hungry?"

"Yes, Mistress."

"Good, I brought you something," she squeezed her thighs feeling the warm stickiness inside, "leftovers from lunch."

Saturday morning was like all recent mornings, Gary cooking breakfast, serving and cleaning up. It was now assumed that he did all the domestic household duties, which kept him quite busy and left him virtually no free time. Joanna, on the other hand, was living a life of luxury: reading, chatting on the phone, going to the club to play tennis or the gym to work out, and going out in the evenings to - well, it wasn't Gary's place to know.

He was wiping the counter when he heard the bell and scurried to answer its call. He didn't run, Joanna had told him, "Sissy maids don't run, they scurry, mince, or crawl."

He arrived in the living room and curtsied.

Joanna didn't even look at him, but said, "Ashtray." There was an ashtray just beyond her reach, she could have easily got it for herself, but this was about training, discipline and conditioning.

Gary wordlessly moved the ashtray to a place convenient for Mistress Joanna, curtsied and backed out of the room.

Joanna didn't watch him leave, only smiled to herself and flicked an ash in the ashtray, *excellent.*

Twenty minutes later she rang the bell again and just as expected Gary quickly appeared. "Your new bedroom furniture is being delivered this afternoon. I think the trim in your bedroom needs another coat of paint. Change into your work clothes and do that. Now."

Gary retrieved the paint and tools from the basement and changed into his work clothes: the pink and purple lace trimmed cut-off coveralls, pink gloves and high-heeled work boots. He hoped he would be able to finish the painting before the deliverymen arrived with his new furniture, but Joanna had purposely cut his time window very short. He worked quickly but neatly, in Mistress Joanna's household any mistake resulted in either a humiliating or painful punishment, sometimes both.

He'd been working for over an hour and was not yet half finished when the doorbell rang. Joanna answered the door and he heard talking and men's voices: "... furniture... delivery... bed... upstairs..." Suddenly there were footsteps coming up the stairs and Joanna's voice, "I'll show you the room and you can decide how you want to bring it all in."

She appeared at the door, accompanied by three burly delivery men. "Still painting, dear? I'd thought you would have finished by now," she smirked. "Let these nice men take a look at your room. They're going to bring up your new furniture."

Gary stood, quiet, his eyes downcast, cheeks flushed with shame.

"He's a bit shy," Joanna teased. "But he's so excited about his new room."

The taller of the men gave Gary a long look. "He lives here? It's a he, right? This is your husband, no offense at my tone."

"Oh, none taken," Karin smiled. "This is my domestic servant, he keeps house, cooks, clean."

"Sort of like a maid," the man said.

"Exactly."

"Yea, OK, whatever. And that bed and stuff, it goes up here, it's his? 'Cause we thought it was like for a little girl's room."

"Oh, it's all for him."

He shrugged. "OK guys, let's bring it up."

"Dear, why don't you get these men something to drink? Would you men like some refreshments? It's really no trouble for him at all."

"Sure thanks, Lady, if it's no trouble."

"No trouble," Karin laughed, "I mean, I'm certainly not the one who has to do it."

Gary prepared and served cold drinks as the men brought up and assembled the furniture. When he saw the man unpacking and setting up the bedroom the nature of their initial confusion became clear. Joanna had selected white furniture with gold accents, very girly and feminine in décor. And the bed was a four-poster with a canopy, a pink canopy.

When the last piece of plastic and cardboard had been removed, the deliveryman asked Joanna to sign for the set-up. "Everything OK, Ma'am?"

"Oh yes, thank you. It looks wonderful; I know he'll be very happy here." She handed the man a twenty dollar bill.

"Thanks Ma'am, appreciate it."

Joanna turned to Gary. "Aren't you going to tip the gentleman?"

Gary stood, confused, he had no money.

Joanna whispered in the deliveryman's ear.

With an evil grin he turned to Joanna, "Really?"

Joanna nodded; and the man quickly unzipped

his pants and leered at Gary.

Gary glanced at Joanna to see her eyes were evil slits and her mouth curled into a feral smile. She simply nodded and watched as Gary dropped to his knees and crawled across the carpet to the deliveryman.

Over the next week Joanna continued her subjugation of Gary. With every instance he became more compliant and submissive and she more fully embraced her dominance and superiority.

One evening after supper she summoned him to her home office.

"Yes, Mistress?"

"Kneel here," she pointed to the floor by her desk, "we need to go over some things." She produced a stack of papers. "Sign this one, here."

"Yes, Mistress, but what are..."

The slap came so fast and so hard it knocked him off his knees and onto the floor.

"Want to try again, bitch?" Joanna growled. "Get up and sign."

Shaking, and with tears in his eyes, Gary took the pen and signed on the line.

For the next twenty minutes Joanna produced papers and documents of various shapes, sizes and thicknesses, demanding Gary's signature on this line or that line, initialing and dating.

When she finished she locked the papers in her safe. Her final act was to open a drawer and produce his wallet. She dumped the contents on her desk. With gleeful malice she handed him a pair of scissors and one of his credit cards. "Cut it up," she ordered.

Gary cut the card up into small pieces and dropped them in a wastepaper basket. Joanna handed him another of his credit cards. Slowly she went through the contents of his wallet: credit cards, library card, gym membership until nearly everything was gone.

"There's not really much you need," she offered, "driver's license, medical and car insurance cards. I'm leaving you one credit card, but I'll be watching it, so don't use it unless you have my permission. Here's a photo to keep with you."

The picture was of Joanna and a good looking man. Both were dressed very well as if on a night on the town.

"What do you say?"

"Thank you, Mistress."

"Go to your room now."

Gary rose without a word, curtsied, backed out of Joanna's office and walked down the hall to his maid's room with the pretty canopy bed.

Joanna picked up her cell phone to call her mentor in domination. "Karin, I did it, I own his ass, hell, I own everything now."

"Really, it hasn't even been two weeks."

"I know, but it's like you said, it must be his

nature, who, or what, he is inside. Tomorrow I'm going to see that friend of yours, that Notary, and have her make everything legal."

"It all sounds wonderful"

"And how are you and Suzette doing?"

Karin shifted her weight and lifted her bottom, hearing the wet and mangled face below gasp a breath of fresh air. "We are having the best of times, thank you for asking."

"I want you to start exercising," Joanna said, "every day." She saw the confused look on Gary's face, "What?"

"Mistress, there's no time, when I get home from work I..."

"I think the sluttier you get the dumber you get! That's why I'm doing all the thinking for us. Of course you don't have time at night. Duh!" Joanna handed him a gift wrapped box. "I spoil you, I don't know why, but I do. Open it."

Gary peeled off the pink ribbon, *why is everything pink anymore* and opened the lid. Inside he found a pink leotard, pink patent five inch heels and a selection of videos. "Thank you, Mistress."

Joanna ignored his thanks. "Here's your schedule, Monday through Friday you'll get up at five a.m. and do one of these exercise videos. You will always wear your leotards and the heels. On Monday, Wednesday and Friday you will do the Sexy Dance Aerobics Workout, on Tuesday you will do the Belly Dance video and on Thursday you will do the Strip Tease Exercise Video. That and your new diet will help you get in shape."

"Diet?"

"Slim Trim shakes for breakfast and lunch and one for supper, plus you can have any scraps from my plate. You do want to be a pretty little slut, don't you?"

"Yes, Mistress."

Gary was late for work; it was taking longer each day to get ready. There seemed to be an ever-increasing list of tasks he had to complete each morning and Joanna was always adding some new wrinkle to make his daily life uncomfortable. First it had been wearing women's panties to work; that hadn't been bad, he could simply slip them on and they actually felt rather nice. Then she escalated to bras, pantyhose, garter belts and stockings, a bit of mascara, some peach eye shadow. They were all little things, but they took more and more time each day to accomplish, as if work life itself hadn't become hell enough with his new hairdo, eyebrows and earrings.

Several of his co-workers had stopped talking to him, although one or two men had become friendlier as of late, even inviting him to lunch. Several of the women in the office had confided how they appreciated the way he was in touch with 'fashion' and his 'feminine side.'

He grabbed his briefcase and his Slim Trim shake for lunch. Joanna weighed him constantly and he was punished if he wasn't making progress to whatever goal she had in mind.

For the third time he rummaged through the living room.

"What are you looking for?" demanded Joanna.

He stopped and bobbed a curtsey, even thought he was dressed conventionally, for work, "My keys Mistress, the keys to my truck."

"They're on the counter."

He looked at the keys on the counter but couldn't recognize them. "No, Mistress, my keys, the keys -"

"Those ARE your keys," Joanna barked.

He flinched at the tone and picked up the keys. He recognized the house key, but the car key was for a Volkswagen. And the key ring itself was pink with a pink "puff" on it and a small purple kitty cat. He had that dazed and confused look that Joanna was coming to love.

"That's for your car; I traded in your truck. Sissies don't drive trucks. Check out your new ride baby," she taunted.

Gary nervously went to the front door and opened it. Sitting in the driveway was a purple Volkswagen Beetle.

"Of course, it's an automatic, no need for you

to have to mess with all that complicated shifting. It has a bud vase, isn't that cute? I expect you to always have a fresh flower in there. Well?"

He turned, totally defeated and crushed. His cock was in chastity, his wallet bare, his hair streaked and eyebrows arched, clad in women's undergarments and driving to work in a chick car. "It's very nice Mistress, thank you."

"Run along to work now."

That afternoon Karin settled back into her Jacuzzi tub and sipped her wine. Life was good and getting better. She picked up the phone. "Karin - yes - I think we're there. Yes, he saw the car. Nothing, he didn't say anything but "thank you" and he went to work. I agree, I think he's ready. It's time that our new sissy maid gets a formal introduction to Master Brent."

Eleven

Joanna fussed with the bow in his hair, pulling and tugging until the pink and white lace took the prescribed shape. Backing away she smiled. "Very pretty. Let's hope Master will be pleased."

Gary groaned. This evening's meeting was to be yet another test, another humiliation for a submissive, feminized, cuckolded husband. It wasn't enough that she cuckolded him, now he was to become a willing participant, a simpering, mincing sissy maid to serve both Mistress and Master.

Joanna switched on her digital camera. "Model for me, hands on hips, quarter turns, stomach in, titties out, and smile!"

Gary turned, remembering to keep his feet close together. Perched on the five inch stilettos, standing ankle to ankle, he slowly turned, trying to strike the requisite pose and please Mistress.

The sight excited and amused her. Now her husband in name only, the sissified creature had become a mere servant and maid. His outfit was made to expose, torment and humiliate. Her maid wore a short black dress, flared almost horizontal by billowing white petticoats. Seamed fishnet stockings were secured to garters hanging from the rigid, steel-boned corset that nipped in his waist. A short black page boy wig framed a face with whorish, 'I'm-a-fuck-me-slut' makeup. The pretty pink and white hair bow matched the delicate lace choker around his neck.

"Dress up!" Joanna ordered.

Gary grabbed the hem with a delicate thumb and forefinger and gently lifted his dress.

Joanna rose from her chair and approached, her hand grasping the plastic prison that entombed his cock. She twisted and pulled, ensuring the security of the device. "Best we keep this locked up."

"Yes, Mistress," he softly replied.

"It's no good to me, other than to tease or torment. It's useless to pleasure a woman."

"Yes, Mistress."

"And keeping it locked up keeps you from wasting valuable time by playing with it."

"Yes, Mistress." He could barely remember the last time he'd been allowed to touch his cock.

"Now Brent," she purred, "he's got a real cock, the kind that can please a woman." She let the chastised member disdainfully drop from her hand. "Finish your dusting, Master will be here soon."

The doorbell rang promptly at seven and they both went to the door. Joanna stood back as Gary opened the door.

Gary curtsied and softly said, "Welcome to Mistress Joanna's home, please come in."

Brent walked in and waited while Gary closed the door and took his coat. Even in five inch heels Gary was dwarfed by the six foot five Master Brent.

Brent walked to Joanna and swept her up in his arms for a deep and sensuous kiss.

This torrid display, his wife flaunting her infidelity and sexuality so openly, shamed and humiliated Gary; but at the same time his flaccid penis tried to erect in the confining plastic tube.

Joanna broke the kiss and reached over to lift up Gary's dress. "Look, the little sissy is turned on. Does it excite you, to see me with a real man?"

Unable to meet her eyes he haltingly replied, "Yes, Mistress."

Brent approached the sissified thing, "So this is our little maid? She looks quite the slut, Joanna. Are you?" he asked Gary. "Are you our little slut, our sissy maid?"

He knew the expected response and curtsied, "Yes, Master."

Brent turned to Joanna. "What do we call her?"

Joanna licked her lips at the erotic scene of dominance and submission playing out before her. "I've been considering that. How about Donna, isn't that a delightful name?"

Brent circled the trembling Gary, taking it all in, making a careful appraisal of the simpering creature before him. "Donna, yes I like it. How high are these heels?"

"Five inches," Joanna replied.

"Hmm, I never want to see her in anything less than four inches, preferably higher, the higher the better."

Joanna beamed. "Oh she loves wearing the highest of heels don't you - Donna?"

Gary, now 'Donna' could only nod in the affirmative. His wife and lover were talking about him as if he were a thing, not even there.

Master Brent continued his inspection. "I want her mouth open, always, like she's hungry for a cock, or ready to deep-throat Mistress's stiletto. Open your mouth sissy, lick those lips, make that tongue sexy and inviting."

Gary flashed a memory of being in the cage, sucking Master Brent's cock, and opened his mouth, running his tongue sensuously over his lips, trying his best to look sexy and seductive.

Master seemed pleased. "Yes, do that always; your mouth should be continually advertising itself as a welcome receptacle for whatever a Master or Mistress wants to insert." He turned to Joanna, "Is her ass plugged?"

Joanna gleefully smiled and nodded. "Bend

over - Donna!" she barked.

Gary bent at the waist, lifting the dress and petticoats to expose his ass, filled with a large pink butt plug.

Brent pushed on the plug, causing Gary to gasp and delighting both Mistress and Master. Brent nodded his approval. "Very nice, I want her always lubed and ready to be used."

"Up!" Joanna commanded.

Gary rose, but kept his hands clasped behind his back and his eyes on the floor.

"You don't think her makeup is too much?" Joanna asked.

"It's good, but more is better. Lots of eye makeup. Can we get her eyelashes longer?"

Joanna considered the question. "There's an on-line site, mostly for erotic dancers and strippers that has hideously long ones."

"Perfect, do that. When she's sucking my cock I want to see her looking up at me through long fluttering eyelashes."

Joanna laughed at the thought of Gary sucking a huge cock and looking up at Master with adoring and appreciative eyes.

"No pantyhose," Brent continued, "stockings only, with seams."

Joanna pulled close to Brent, her tongue sensuously licking his neck. "Oh lover, this is so wicked."

Brent's hand disappeared into Donna's dress and grabbed a nipple.

Gary winced and buckled at the knees.

Brent gave Joanna a questioning look.

Joanna licked his ear and whispered, "She loves to have her nipples played with."

With a wicked smile Brent continued his assault on Donna's tender nipples. "Well let's not deny the poor creature. All of her service outfits will show her exposed nipples."

Joanna's hand snaked down to Brent's crotch as she stroked his growing cock. "Oh baby, you are so wicked. This will be so much fun."

"Yes, with the changes I've outlined I approve of our little sissy Donna. With some training and discipline she'll make a fine Sissy Maid."

"Oh darling, I'm thrilled you approve." Joanna turned to the hapless creature before her. "You will serve us wine in the living room, light the candles in my bedroom and turn down the bed. And before you come back downstairs change into your six inch heels and put on another coat of mascara." Arm-in-arm Master and Mistress walked to the living room, while Donna curtsied and minced off to do their bidding.

All-in-all, thought Joanna, *the formal introduction went quite well.*

Twelve

Don't you look precious?" Joanna mewed.

Gazing at his reflection in the mirror Gary didn't think so. The impending humiliation of an evening spent dressed as a serving maid to friends and work colleagues was unnerving.

Joanna held out a pair of pink elbow-length gloves. Gary, now Donna, dutifully curtsied, took the gloves and began putting them on.

"Really sweetheart, you do look very much the adorable sissy. Everyone will be quite amused," Joanna mocked.

Gary's curtsey and "Yes, Ma'am," wasn't all that convincing, but the thought of another session in the cage made almost anything bearable. Gary rolled the last glove up his arm and looked at the image in the mirror. Yes, Donna was very much the sissy. She wore the short black maid's dress, now with the titty cut-outs favored by Master Brent. This particular dress was trimmed in pink lace, with a dainty pink apron. The pink gloves, lace choker and pink lace headband completed the look. A boned and tightly cinched corset gave a pleasing hour-glass shape and ensured a most correct posture. Garters from the corset held up the black seamed stockings that Master Brent found so alluring. *I like to dress sexy for men* the mantra from the cage sounded in sissy's head. *If I please Master, he will please Mistress and I will have done my job as a sissy maid.*

Donna's feet were crammed into black patent, pointed-toe stilettos with six-inch heels. These forced the short, delicate steps that were the hallmark of a mincing sissy maid. The black page boy wig was standard maid wear and Joanna had abetted the look with the hideously long false eye lashes and extreme makeup.

"One last touch," Joanna said, as she reached up and clipped long, seven-inch earrings to Donna's ears. "Move your head!"

Donna moved her head side to side, the heavy earrings pulling at the earlobes.

"Lovely," Joanna exclaimed. "They catch the light beautifully. Open," she said, holding out a pill.

Donna opened her mouth to swallow the pill.

Joanna lifted up sissy's dress and pink petticoats and fondled the 'sissy clit' enclosed in the plastic chastity device. "Just a little Viagra to get you through the night; try not to get too excited dear, it's liable to be painful and frustrating. Remember, Master Brent wants to see that sexy little mouth open all night. There's likely to be a lot of real man cocks looking for a slut fuck hole. Is your bottom lubed?"

"Yes, Mistress."

"Very well, go and finish your preparations in the kitchen. When the guests arrive answer the door and greet them. Be polite and do whatever you are told."

"Yes, Mistress." Donna curtsied, backed away and teetered off to the kitchen on her stiletto heels.

Everything was ready for Mistress's dinner party and Donna was polishing the ashtrays for the third time when the doorbell rang. The first guest was Karin's friend Sheila Remington. Donna took Sheila's hat and coat and stood while Sheila inspected Donna's chastity device. Guests continued to arrive, both singles and couples. Donna greeted each with a delicate curtsey and a "Welcome to Mistress Joanna's home."

The guests took whatever liberties they wanted with the domestic help and Donna was subjected to a variety of shoe and boot licking, nipple torments and ass kissing. A table near the door held a satin-lined wicker basket full of clothespins. Guests were free to place them wherever they wanted and Donna soon found them fastened to her nipples, ears, tongue, wherever a guest felt inclined. A guest would attach one and another guest may later remove it, or change its position.

When Gary's boss from work, Karl Devlin, arrived Joanna ran up to give him a long kiss. As they kissed, Devlin ran his hands up and down Joanna's body, cupping her ass and fondling her breasts. Joanna broke the kiss and stepped back, her finger tracing a line down his chest to his crotch, "Karl, so good of you to come. Donna has been so anxious to see you, haven't you sissy?"

Donna knew the answer expected. With shame and humiliation burning her face she curtsied to her employer and boss. "Welcome to Mistress Joanna's home, Master Karl."

Devlin shook his head in amazement. "Damn, Joanna! I know we were getting it on in my office while this pathetic little shit worked on his spreadsheets down the hall, but this, this..."

Joanna moved in front of Devlin and pulled his arms around her. She placed his hands on her breasts, and he caressed the magnificent globes, barely contained by her low-cut evening dress. Leaning her head back Joanna invited his kisses to her neck.

Gary felt his imprisoned cock try vainly to

erect. His wife and his boss were getting it on right in front of him and he was getting excited. *Joanna is right; I must be a natural cuckold sissy. And Master Brent hasn't even arrived yet!*

Devlin removed his lips from Joanna's neck and smiled. "Maybe we could find her a new job at work, as a secretary or an office girl?"

Gary shuddered at the thought of full exposure and humiliation at his workplace.

"Not yet," Joanna cautioned. "I still like the money he brings in. But there's no reason some of his daily duties and responsibilities couldn't change or be increased: making and fetching coffee for the secretaries, filing and copying, picking up their dry cleaning."

"I'm sure that can be arranged," Devlin laughed. Arm-in-arm he and Joanna walked into the living room, leaving Donna to struggle with a frustrated erection and absolute humiliation.

Guests continued to arrive and visit torments on her. One of the last guests was an elderly woman accompanied by a lovely young girl. The older woman was distinguished looking, with perfectly coifed silver hair and a beautiful evening dress. The young girl's nervous eyes peered out from under a short black page boy hair style and she was garishly made up, as was Donna.

Joanna rushed up to greet the older woman, embracing her. "Margaret, so good of you to come. And this must be little Prissy. Donna! Come and meet Mistress Margaret and Prissy."

Donna minced over to deliver the customary

curtsey and greeting while Margaret observed it all in a desultory manner. "Acceptable, Joanna, she seems to be a serviceable piece of merchandise. Shall we introduce our sissies?"

"By all means," Joanna said, "by all means."

With a flourish Margaret removed her slave's coat, "Sissy Donna, meet sissy Prissy!"

As the room burst into laughter and applause Donna realized that all the guests had gathered around them. To the laughter of the assembled crowd she took in the image of the submissive standing before her. Prissy wore an outfit identical to Donna's, except for the reversal of the colors. Prissy's dress was pink with black lace trim and she wore black gloves. Both sissies wore identical stockings, shoes, wigs and makeup.

"Stand together girls, side by side, arms around each other," Joanna barked.

The two sissies shuffled in place, eyes downcast, their faces flushed with humiliation.

Joanna raised her glass in a toast and announced, "I give you Donna and Prissy, our sissy twins for the evening."

Everyone laughed and clapped as the two sissies unconsciously huddled closer together, seeking a refuge they knew did not exist.

Joanna was feeling it now, the heady power over her hapless, submissive, sissified husband. How low could she take him? With an elegantly manicured nail she lifted her husband's painted face to look him in the eyes. "Do you think Prissy is pretty?" she asked.

Dropping into a curtsey Donna replied, "Yes Ma'am, Prissy is very pretty."

"Then tell her how pretty she is and give her a nice big sissy kiss."

Gary felt his knees go weak. Joanna was going to make him kiss another man, in front of everyone. The room was alive with comments: 'A sissy kiss, a sissy kiss!' 'Is her husband gay?' 'No, that's what makes it so delicious.' 'Ann! Ann, over here, it's a sissy kiss.'

Joanna was losing her patience. "Well, what's the problem? I want to see a sexy sissy kiss. You're not men, or even boys, you're sissies, so go ahead and kiss. We're all waiting. Tell Prissy how pretty she is and give her a big kiss."

The two sissies turned to face each other, putting their arms around one another.

"You look very pretty tonight Prissy."

"Thank you," Prissy answered. "You look very pretty too."

Both sissies leaned in, their open mouths making contact, tongues intertwined, exploring, tasting. Their gloved hands clutched each other's body.

Joanna toasted her power with a long drink of Champagne and turned to the embracing sissies. "Keep kissing, but play with each other's titties."

As the sissies kissed and fondled titties, cameras flashed around the room as guests recorded the event. Two guests circled the entwined sissies capturing their lust on video.

Devlin finished taking his digital pictures and

returned the camera to his pocket. Joanna slid next to him and gave him a kiss.

"If he doesn't want those pictures making the rounds at the office I think he'll do whatever we say," Devlin said.

"Baby," Joanna purred, "we got him right where we want him. OK sissies, that's enough!"

The two sissies broke the kiss and stood side by side.

"Out to the kitchen," Joanna ordered. "There's a lot of serving to do."

While the superior Mistresses and Masters mingled, chatted and enjoyed drinks the two submissive sissies minced precariously about on their six inch heels carrying trays of drinks and food, lighting cigarettes and emptying ash trays. More than once a guest would casually flick an ash to the floor and watch with bemusement as the nearest sissy quickly fell to her knees to lap it up.

The guests amused themselves by fondling the exposed titties, asses, or plastic-encased sissy clits. By the time the guests assembled for dinner the sissies' nipples were tender and sore, their balls aching from constant groping and their Viagra-infused sissy clits straining in useless frustration in their plastic confines. Both sissies knew better than to complain, or let such things impair their service. Their lot was to endure, serve and entertain. None of this was made any easier by the high heels or restrictive corsets, but such attire pleased their superiors. With the guests seated for dinner Joanna ordered the service to begin.

Prissy and Donna teetered from kitchen to dining room, serving each course, clearing plates and filling water and wine glasses. Bending low, as was instructed, to serve each course, the sissies were routinely groped and manhandled. It was not uncommon for a guest on each side to grasp a tender nipple between their thumb and forefinger, pinching, pulling and twisting the nub. The girls were expected to hold their position and endure in silence. Their asses were slapped and pinched and their balls groped, all amid polite dinner conversation by the assembled guests. They were kept in constant motion and service for the two-hour dinner, scurrying between kitchen and dining room, serving their Masters and Mistresses. There were no breaks and relief, constant service being the only consideration.

At the conclusion of the feast Joanna suggested they all retire to the Great Room for coffee and Cognac. Again the sissies circulated the room, serving coffee, pouring Cognac, lighting cigarettes and proffering humidors of cigars for the gentlemen. After everyone's needs were met Joanna dismissed the sissy twins to clean up the dining room and kitchen. Still not allowed any rest or chance to get off their aching feet, Joanna did allow them to, "Help yourselves to the scraps from our plates."

In the kitchen the sissies worked and talked in hushed tones. "You're Mistress Joanna's husband?" Prissy asked.

"In name only, on the marriage license," Gary answered ruefully.

"Now you're her sissy maid." It was said as a statement of fact, not a question. "How did it happen?"

Gary shrugged. "Games, I guess. I'd always wanted to try BDSM, some Fem Dom things. And one day Mistress met this woman - and they changed me."

Prissy nodded knowingly; it wasn't an uncommon story. Once one started down the path, once a woman found the power and rush of domination, once a man came to face his submissive tendencies it often ended up like this. "Do you like dressing up?"

Gary hesitated for a moment, listening for the voice. *I like to wear high heels. I want to dress pretty for men. Wearing makeup is fun.* "Yes."

"Me too, it makes me feel sexy. But it still bothers you a bit?"

"Sometimes; I like the feel of the clothes and shoes, but sometimes I'm embarrassed."

"They like that, to embarrass us." She put a gloved hand on Donna's arm. "It gets easier with time."

"And you? You're much younger than Mistress Margaret."

Prissy paused and sighed, "She bought me..."

The tinkling of a crystal bell caught the sissies' attention and hand-in-hand they scurried to the Great Room.

"Aren't they precious?"

"So sweet."

"Joanna, he's so obedient."

"She," Joanna reminded.

"Look at those hungry little mouths."

"Time for some entertainment," Joanna said. "On your hands and knees girls, in front of the machines."

In the center of the room two fucking machines faced each other, their heavy steel shafts containing ten-inch dildos. The two sissies assumed positions on their hands and knees, their faces nearly touching, the loathsome dildos nudging their puckered sissy pussies.

Joanna held up a remote control. "Now girls, I want you to kiss each other while the machines give your sissy pussies a good fucking."

Margaret approached the two sissies and opened her hand to reveal nipple clamps attached to a short length of chain, with a sterling silver bell dangling from each clamp. She bent down, pinching and pulling each sissy nipple until the clamps were firmly attached. When she finished, the two sissies were tethered by their nipples, the taut chains painfully pulling at the slightest movement.

"Wonderful," beamed Joanna as she pressed START on the remote. The dildos began their relentless and rhythmic penetration, each sissy gasping as they were impaled by the latex intruder. Their nipples were painfully distended as they rocked to the rhythm of the machines, the silver bells adding a merry ring to the relentless drone of the fucking machines.

"Kiss," Joanna ordered, "you're supposed to be entertaining us. Make it sexy and slutty."

To the tinkling of the bells and the gasps and moans of the kneeling figures, the Dominants in the room talked of books, movies and current events, casting only the occasional eye to the sweating, panting sissies on the floor beneath them.

Thirteen

Preparing and serving the Sunday morning breakfast to Mistress and Master had taken Donna longer than usual. The cleanup was laborious as well. Mistress had decided that Donna had been "too fidgety" in her cage the previous evening, and as punishment had hobbled her ankles with an eight inch chain.

Donna couldn't help but fidget in the cage. Mistress had kept her in the tortuous six-inch heels all night. It was impossible to get comfortable in her cage with the killer spike heels locked on all night. Now she minced about the kitchen, each tiny step agony on her feet and calves. She'd been in the dreaded shoes for over thirty six hours! When the last plate was dried and put away she made the agonizing walk to the sun room, to report to Mistress and Master.

Teetering before Mistress, Donna curtsied as gracefully as possible given her short ankle hobble.

Joanna looked up from her Sunday newspaper supplement. "I hope you've learned your lesson."

Unable to speak, Donna mutely nodded. In addition to being hobbled Mistress had made her wear the dreaded penis gag when she'd been released from the cage. Her mouth ached and the drool running down her chin was another embarrassing humiliation.

Karin put out her cigarette. "I bet you'd like that gag off."

Donna nodded, her eyes pleading for relief from the plastic phallus that invaded and stretched her mouth.

"Come here then."

Donna shuffled forward and offered her head to Mistress.

Joanna took a small key from her robe pocket, unlocked and removed the gag.

Free of the intruder Donna took a deep breath and stretched her jaw.

"The shoes and the hobbles stay on," Joanna ordered.

Her halting curtsey was Donna's routine acknowledgement of an order by a superior.

"Slut!" Master Brent said.

Donna turned and curtsied, dismayed to find Master Brent casually folding back his robe to expose his impressive cock. Donna saw Mistress give her cruel smile. They'd removed the horrid gag only to replace it with something larger, more invasive, more demeaning.

Karin nodded towards Brent, a non-verbal order for a sissy to get about her task.

Dismayed, Donna shuffled before Master, and fell to her knees, between his spread legs. She'd been well coached on providing this service. The first task was to beg to suck the cock. Mistress had explained it thus, "Real men like it when a slut gets on her knees and begs to suck their cock. They like to hear it in her voice and see it in her eyes."

The properly trained sissy began. "Master, may I please suck your cock? It feels so good in my mouth. I love it when it gets big and hard and fills my sissy mouth. It tastes so good when I lick and suck it. Please Master, please put your big cock in this slut's face fuck hole."

Joanna smiled proudly at her sissy's pleading, self-degradation. Even Brent turned and smiled his approval at the groveling.

Master reached down and grabbed his cock, already starting to erect at the mere thought of face fucking the kneeling slut. Holding his cock he slapped sissy's face with it, back and forth, the dull 'thwack' of the cock on the face bringing laughter to Master and Mistress. When he tired of the phallic face pummeling Master teased sissy's mouth with his cock.

Donna knew the drill and begged in earnest. "Please, Master, let me suck your cock."

"Shit!" Joanna exclaimed. "I'm tired of listening to her incessant begging. Fuck the slut's face and shut her up."

Brent grabbed the back of Donna's head and slowly pulled the tender slut mouth down his shaft. He kept her there until she gagged then released her, just a bit. "Nice and gentle," he ordered. "Give me a nice, long and gentle cock sucking while I read the paper." Without another word he threw his robe closed, covering his crotch and the kneeling sissy beneath. He and Joanna returned to their Sunday papers, while between Brent's legs, Donna made slow, sensuous love to Master's cock.

Twenty minutes into the task Master suddenly threw back the robe, exposing the sissy below. Looking down he saw their sissy, her mouth full of real man cock, licking and slurping away, her adoring eyes looking up through the hideously long, fluttering eyelashes.

That was another of Joanna's edicts of oral service for sissy maids. "When orally pleasing a man always look up at him with adoring eyes, let him see how much you love his cock and appreciate him letting you suck it."

"Joanna," asked Brent, "what do you think about having all her teeth removed?"

"I'd really never given it any thought," said Joanna as she turned a page in the Lifestyle section. "Exactly what do you have in mind?"

"Think how convenient it would be for cock sucking, no teeth, no biting, no scratching."

"Yes, there is that, I suppose."

Brent continued. "There's really not that much of a reason for her to have intelligible speech and as for eating, a simple gruel or liquid diet could suffice."

"All good points, yes. But I was thinking of hiring her out as a she-male escort for gay men. You said you have some gay colleagues at work and your boss is such a stickler for male-female only couples at his functions. Sissy here is the perfect answer, a cover date for your gay friends to take to office functions. And you have to admit, a toothless slut in a cocktail dress is not the perfect date, at least not until after the party."

Donna cast nervous eyes to Mistress, was rewarded with a slap on the head and a "focus!" from Master and quickly returned her full attention to the cock in her mouth.

"Yes, I'd forgotten about that," Brent agreed. "Alex in Accounting is very keen on doing our little slut. I do have a good acquaintance, a dentist friend. He might be inclined to remove her teeth and fit her with some dazzling white dentures to show off against some fire-engine red fuck-me lips. He's a bit of a scene player himself; he might actually do it for free if he could take it out in trade, so to speak."

Karin smiled, considering it. "Hmm, it does have possibilities, but for now we'll forego it. But if she continues to misbehave, or her performance is lacking, it might be just the thing to bring her in line."

Both Mistress and Master laughed sending a chill through Donna.

Brent dropped his paper and grabbed Donna's head in his massive hands. "OK slut, I think I'm ready to come so get to work down there and bring me off. And be sure to swallow every drop like a good girl."

Fourteen

Donna dropped the dish towel and ran for the door as soon as she heard Mistress Joanna's car pull in the garage. She took a quick moment to straighten her dress and apron and brushed a stray lock of hair out of her face. Mistress was a stickler for perfect appearance and punishments for non-compliance were swift and harsh. She listened carefully, judged when Joanna was near the door and opened it, performing the small bob curtsey of greeting and respect.

Joanna breezed through the door, dropping her purse on the counter. "Get the packages, take them to my bedroom and bring me a drink."

Donna bobbed in acknowledgement, but Joanna had already left the room, ignoring her submissive maid. In the recesses of her mind Donna heard the voice, *I must obey* and minced into the garage on her stiletto heels to do her Mistress's bidding.

Mistress had been on quite a shopping spree and it took Donna two trips to get all the packages to Joanna's bedroom. Finished with that task, she prepared a Vodka Martini, placed it on the silver tray and delivered it to Joanna.

"You finished the cleaning?" asked Joanna as she accepted the drink.

"Yes, Mistress."

Joanna picked up a cigarette and Donna immediately produced a lighter from her apron pocket. "You took the packages to my bedroom?"

"Yes, Mistress."

"Rub my feet."

Donna knelt and carefully removed Joanna's high heeled pumps. As she had been trained, she began to gently knead and massage the soles of Mistress's feet. Bending forward she inhaled the aroma of the foot: an intoxicating mixture of lotion, leather and sweat; sissy ambrosia.

Joanna looked down on her maid, servant, sex slave, toy and - oh yes - husband. Karin had certainly altered that particular relationship dynamic. And now Joanna was going to take it one step further. She took a drag on her cigarette and smiled. *This is going to be fun.* "We're going out this weekend, on Saturday night, a date."

Although it broke submissive protocol Donna looked up with surprise. While Mistress went out often with other men it had been weeks since they'd been anywhere as husband and wife.

"Yes, it's a dinner party, very formal, I'll be dressed in a beautiful gown and gloves, you'd like that wouldn't you?"

"Oh yes, Mistress, I'd be very happy to escort you."

"We have all week to get ready." *All week to make you into the perfect date.* Joanna held out the empty Martini glass. *One more drink and then we get to work.*

Donna shifted nervously, hoping Mistress Joanna wouldn't notice.

"Stay still!" Joanna barked.

Being still wasn't easy. Donna's kneeling place was on the hardwood floor, in the corner, which Mistress Joanna had liberally strewn with uncooked rice and peas. It was such a simple thing, but it caused a most delectable torment.

Joanna twirled holding a black evening gown. "What do you think of this? I love the way it dips in the back. It's so sexy!"

"Yes, Mistress, it's very beautiful. You'll look very sexy."

"And with these gloves," Joanna said, as she held up an exquisite pair of elbow-length, black kid-leather gloves. *Now the good part.* She looked directly at Donna. "Brent will love this!"

Donna's expression went blank, unable to figure out what Joanna meant.

"Brent, he's my date this weekend. You look confused. Do you have a question? Speak."

"I thought I was going to the party with you Mistress."

"You are darling, of course you are." *Still confused, maybe Karin kept her in that cage too long. Oh well, simple works best for her now.* "Brent is my date for the party and Alex is your date."

The shock, fear and surprise on Donna's face were exactly what Joanna wanted.

"Yes, dear. Brent's boss, Mr. Stearns, is hosting a dinner party for his executive staff and I'm Brent's date. Brent's co-worker Alex is gay and Sterns has a 'thing' about only male-female couples at his formal, corporate parties. Although I'm given to believe that he hosts other parties where anything goes. Why he'd fire Alex if he arrived at a corporate function with a man in tow. So you're going as Alex's date." *The look on her poor face is priceless.* "Do you want to see what I picked out for you to wear?"

The pain in Donna's knees was now replaced by a pain in the gut, the fear and humiliation of being pimped out as a gay date.

Joanna's smile was one of genuine glee, if a bit wicked. She pulled a dress from a shopping bag. "I got you this sexy red dress, very tight, and slit up to here! And look, I also got you some long red gloves, but these have Marabou feathers on the cuffs. Oh and these wicked spike heels. You'll have to learn to dance in the dress and heels. Karin has a friend that she'll send over, a dance teacher. I can't wait to see you out there on the dance floor, grinding your hips, shaking your little booty. You're not happy? Not excited about our double-date? Speak."

"You want me to go as a woman? You want me to be a date for a gay man?"

"You will, I demand it and I expect you to be the perfect date. You're to hold hands with Alex, cuddle, kiss, do whatever you need to do to convince Stearns that Alex has a sexy girlfriend - you. We have all week to get your dress fitted and work on your dancing. Your maid training has given you many of the necessary mannerisms and feminine movements to get you through the evening and we'll augment that with some glamour technique."

Donna reluctantly hung her head in submission and nodded. She heard the voice in her head: *I like to dress sexy for men. Makeup makes me pretty.*

"I'm going to enjoy this, and you do get to go out with me for an evening," Joanna laughed. "It will be our girls' night out; who knows, we might get lucky! Now get up off your knees and put on your outfit; I want to see how pretty you look."

Donna rose to her feet and took the dress, gloves and heels and modeled her date outfit for Joanna, moving, turning and preening at Joanna's directions. "Walk sexy; make short steps, heel-toe, heel-toe. That's better. See how those little steps give you a natural hip swing? OK, pose, hands on hips and look back over your shoulder;

drop the right hip - just a bit. There! That's it."

The dress was skin tight, where it contacted skin, and to Donna's mind that was damned little. It had almost no back and a split up the left side almost to her crotch.

"You'll wear seamed fishnet stockings, very sexy, and a lacy garter belt. Men will be getting a glimpse of that all evening. And you're not to flinch or slap at any hands that may cop a feel. Is that understood?"

"Yes, Mistress."

"We'll have to do something to create a bit more cleavage. There are some very life-like forms that I can glue on. If any men touch you there you need to react like they've touched a real tit, give them a little shake, purse your lips and moan, above all let them know you liked it. And since you can't feel it when someone touches a falsie you need to be paying attention."

"Yes, Mistress."

Joanna circled Donna, satisfied she'd created exactly the right look. "No doubt you'll be dressed sluttier than anyone else there, but that's to Alex's advantage. While Alex's boss is strict about male-female only couples at his corporate functions he's also quite the lecherous devil in his private life. He supposedly has a state of the art dungeon somewhere on his estate. There's no doubt that he'll grope you any chance he gets. But you're to allow that; if you have to whore yourself out to get Alex in good with his boss then you do that. Just don't let Stearns' party guests find out that Alex's date is a man. Questions? Speak."

"Mistress, you mean I'm supposed to let Mr. Stearns fuck me, or what?"

"You're only wearing women's clothes, you haven't got a cunt," Joanna laughed, "so the only thing that's fuckable is your ass." Joanna grabbed Donna's ass and gave it a good groping. "But if you have to let Stearns get back here to keep him happy, well, basically that's your problem to deal with. Bottom line is you need to do what you have to do to please a man, but don't embarrass Alex, or us, or Mr. Stearns. Do I make myself clear?" *She doesn't have much of a choice and the sooner she realizes what she needs to do, the better.*

Donna executed a passable curtsey in the red dress, "Yes, Mistress."

"Trudi will be here every day the rest of this week to help with your dance moves. I want to see you shaking it on the floor, turning on every man in the place. You're Alex's date, but you can't say "no" to any man, got it?"

Again, the voice in her head: *I like to suck cock.* "Yes Mistress, I'm a cock-hungry slut."

Joanna beamed. "Exactly! This is going to be such fun. If you do this well we may double date more often; maybe I can even find you some clients of your own. Let's practice walking in the dress, swish those hips so we can all catch a glimpse of the garter belt and stocking top."

Trudi arrived the next afternoon and Donna immediately fell under the spell and authority of the tall domineering German dance instructress.

"It is not so much dancing we will be working on as moving sexy to the underlying beat of the music," Trudi said. "I will not teach you steps or routines, but how to move for the man, to make him watch you, to make him want you." She put on a CD and the room erupted to a driving four-four techno beat. "This is very popular party music and it gives you much opportunity to do the sexy moves. Stand here, pretend you are the man; pretending, it should not be so hard, ja?" she laughed. "Move your body, back and forth. OK, so that would be the man; let me show you what the woman, what you, will do."

Donna moved back and forth in time to the music while Trudi became a dance vixen. Trudi removed the clip holding her hair and shook the long blonde tresses down to her shoulders, a mane of liquid gold. Her hands moved across her chest, tracing a line between her cleavage and down to her hips. Her pert bottom rotated in time to the music, circling, drawing both the eyes and the lust of her sissified dance partner. She bent at the waist, dropped her head and then flipped it up, her hair Medusa-like, an erotic enticement drawing men to their doom.

She backed into Donna, driving her bottom against the trembling sissy. As she straightened, her hands snaked behind her, tracing inviting lines up Donna's body. Quickly turning, Trudi pulled her hands to her own hips, grinding her pelvis while she sensuously stroked her bottom.

"That is what you will learn," Trudi said as she muted the sound with the stereo remote. "You are dancing for the man, showing him that you want him and what you have to give him. You will tease him, but in the end you will submit to him. These clothes, you will dance in these clothes?"

Donna looked at the maid's day uniform she wore. "No, Mistress bought me a dress and shoes and gloves."

"You will wear those when we practice, your moves and actions will be based on your clothes. Go and change into the clothes you will wear for your date. But first bend over." Trudi walked to an umbrella stand and removed a thin rattan cane. "You will receive six with the cane for not being properly dressed for dance practice."

Donna bent over and meekly pulled up her dress and petticoats. The day uniform garter belt and stockings neatly framed her bottom, making an inviting target for the cane.

Trudi flexed the cane in her hand and lightly tapped it against Donna's buttocks to gauge the distance and select her target. This pre-discipline ritual was quickly concluded and she delivered a deep and wicked stroke to Donna's bottom.

Donna flinched at the pain, hoping that the

pre-caning preparation and ritual might take longer. There was no doubt that Mistress Trudi was a get-down-to-business type. The initial hurt was quickly replaced by the searing bloom of deeper pain. She barely choked out a 'Thank you Mistress' when the second blow landed. Shaking, Donna held her pose; breaking position during discipline always invited extra strokes. The remaining four strikes were delivered in the same precise and disciplined manner and she was shaking and teary-eyed at the end.

Trudi dropped the cane in front of Donna. "Go and change, return in your date clothes in ten minutes or I will cane you a second time."

With genuine gratitude Donna dropped to her knees, kissed the toes of Trudi's high heels and offered a heartfelt, "Thank you, Mistress." She picked up the cane and returned it to the umbrella stand on her way to change clothes.

Fifteen

The week leading to the party was busier than most, not that Donna had any leisure time anyway. Most of her time was taken up with housework, although Mistress Joanna would allow some time to read fashion magazines or watch the Oxygen Channel. She often heard the voices in her head: *Golf is stupid*, *Fashion is fun.*

She endured daily dance lessons with Trudi and Mistress Joanna was pleased when she demonstrated her sexy new moves. She'd received more canings, for poor performance, but Mistress Trudi kept them all high up on the buttocks and not down on the thighs. "Mustn't mark up the sexy thighs we want to show off," Trudi mocked as she wielded the evil cane.

The punishments continued from Mistress Joanna. Not an evening went by that Donna didn't suffer a face slapping or paddling for failing to respond quickly enough or fulfill a task to Joanna's demanding perfection.

In addition to her evening domestic duties and service to Mistress Joanna, Donna spent what little extra time was available practicing the techniques to be a successful date for Alex. She crossed and uncrossed her legs, practiced sitting down and standing up in a sexy manner, and rehearsed standing poses.

Joanna bought an inflatable male love doll and delighted in humiliating Donna by making her nibble on the doll's ear, kiss the doll and hold the doll's arm behind her back and caress her ass. Joanna laughed as she told Donna to rub her bottom against the doll's plastic hard-on. "These are the things you'll have to do," teased Joanna, "if you want to convince everyone that you're Alex's slutty girlfriend."

Donna had no choice but to try her best. If she fucked this up, if Alex wasn't pleased, if someone found out she was a 'man,' if she couldn't satisfy a real man making an advance the consequences would be dire. Joanna had threatened any number of punishments: another session in Karin's cage, a long stay in Trudi's dungeon, or something else too horrible to contemplate.

By Friday Donna was as ready as she could be. After serving lunch and cleaning up the kitchen she was instructed to report to the morning room. When she arrived she found Joanna with a guest.

Joanna nodded to the guest. "This is Madeline, she's a manicurist. She's come to do our nails for the party tonight."

Donna curtsied. "Welcome to Mistress Joanna's house."

"My god, Joanna, she's so cute, so precious." Madeline motioned Donna forward and took one of her hands to give it a cursory inspection. "Yes, we can femme these up."

"Of course she'll be wearing gloves, but when she takes them off I want her date to find some really sexy fingernails." Joanna smiled as she saw Donna blush with the humiliation of being a date for a man.

"So how long do you want them?" Madeline asked.

"At least an inch, preferably longer."

Madeline shook her head. "Wow, that's pretty long. Definitely sexy, no doubt about that, but if she's, is it she or he?"

"She is fine," Joanna smiled.

Madeline laughed, "If she's never worn nails that long it could be a problem."

Joanna paused for a moment. "Well, that will be her little problem, one that she'd better overcome. Put them on, long ones, fire engine red and make sure they stay on." Joanna looked at her own nails. "When you're through with her I'll need a fill and polish."

"No problem, let me get my tools." Madeline turned to give an evil smile to Donna. "Aren't you excited?"

When Madeline finished, Donna held up her hands. Her fingers ended in long red nails. They were securely bonded on; she didn't know when or how they would be removed. She also wasn't sure how she would be able to use her hands.

Joanna removed a large dildo from a drawer. It was ten inches long and two inches in diameter. She thrust it at Donna. "Take it."

Donna hesitantly gripped the large rubber phallus.

"The nails don't stop her from doing that," Madeline laughed.

"Yes," Joanna said, "she'll be able to do the basic and important things. Hold it up to your face and practice walking sexy around the room while your nails dry."

Donna walked around the room, practicing her short heel-toe steps and hip sway while Joanna enjoyed Madeline's expert manicure. Donna's eyes never left the sight of those red talon-like nails wrapped around the thick cock she held before her face.

"Um, she's going to be very popular tonight," Madeline said.

"That's the plan for our little sissy, that's the plan," Joanna smiled.

Late in the afternoon Donna was ordered to take a long scented bubble bath and shave as close as possible. This was a well received luxury and she closed her eyes and relaxed in the warm sweet smelling water. She extended a leg, lathered it up and softly pulled the razor down its length. She smiled as she ran her hand with the sexy red nails over the smooth silken skin. The voices in her head told her that this was right. *It's good to be soft and hairless and I must be pretty for men.*

When she was finished with her bath she wrapped a towel around her head, turban fashion as she had been taught, and toweled herself off. After powdering her freshly shaved body she went to her maid's room and stood by her vanity.

Joanna entered and circled her submissive, running her hands over the naked body. "Very nice, smooth and soft."

Donna bobbed in acknowledgement, her chastised penis bouncing up and down with the action.

"We'll fix that!" Joanna laughed. "Sit facing me!"

Joanna picked up a pair of tweezers, grabbed her sissy's chin and pulled her head up. "I'm doing your eyebrows tonight; I want them to look special."

Unable to curtsey or nod, Donna remained silent and in place.

Joanna worked slowly and steadily, stopping every so often to back up a step and check her work. Donna was turned away from the mirror and had no idea what was happening, other than that there was a lot of plucking going on.

"It's always best to work from the bottom up," lectured Joanna as she tweezed yet another hair, "so as to obtain the best arch. Yes, I like this. We're giving you very sexy eyes this evening. At the party tonight I want you to go to the ladies room every hour and touch up your makeup: add more eyeliner, mascara, lipstick and blush. You may turn around and look in the mirror."

What Donna saw caused her jaw to drop and her eyes to open wide in horror. Her eyebrows had been tweezed to a thin high arch, even more severe than they were after the salon visit. *How can I go to work on Monday like this?*

Joanna could hardly keep from laughing. "Darling what's wrong? I think it looks lovely."

Donna shook her head in despair.

"Speak," Joanna ordered.

"It's so feminine; it won't grow back by Monday."

"Of course it's feminine; you're a sissy and you've got a date tonight silly. And no, it obviously won't grow back by Monday. I like it; you will wear it like this from now on."

Donna nodded, hearing the voice, *I want to have sexy eyes.*

"Now let's start getting you dressed."

Donna submissively allowed Mistress to dress her for her date that night.

Joanna produced a pair of large latex breasts. "We'll have to glue these on, but the adhesive should keep them on throughout the weekend, in case Alex wants to take you home after the party."

A look of terror came over Donna's face.

"What?" asked an irritated Joanna. "You're certainly not dressed as one of those 'goodnight-kiss-at-the-door-types!' If you're going to show it at the party you're going to put out later. Bend over!"

Donna bent over as Joanna grabbed a hair-brush from the table.

"You - need - an - attitude - adjustment - be - fore - this - evening - little - girl!" Between each word Joanna delivered a stinging slap of the hair brush. "You - will - not - fuck - this - up - or - embarrass - me. Do - you - under - stand - me?"

Near sobbing and shaking from both pain and fear Donna moaned. "Yes, I'm sorry, Mistress, I'll be good."

"Go wash your face and dry your eyes, then come back here so we can finish getting you ready."

When Donna returned Joanna held out the breasts and glue. "Lie down on the bed, on your back."

As Donna reclined on the bed Joanna applied a liberal amount of glue to the right artificial breast and to Donna. She carefully positioned the flesh-colored mound and ordered Donna to "hold it in place until it dries." The procedure was repeated for the left breast and Donna was left on the bed holding both breasts in place.

"You little slut," Joanna teased. "It looks like you're feeling yourself up. Lick your lips and practice your 'sexy look' while you hold those until they dry. Alex may want you to play with yourself like that later."

What should have been total shame and embarrassment was instead a sexy and erotic feeling. Donna found herself unconsciously rubbing the fake nipples of her 'breasts' and writing in pleasure as if she could actually feel her fingers stroke the tender little nubs. The voice gave her permission. *Men like to see me play with myself.*

Joanna watched with amazement. *She's a total fucking slut. I bet she'd spend the entire party on her knees crawling from cock to cock if I told her to. Hmm...* She looked at her watch. *Fifteen minutes, the glue should be dry.* "Stand up!"

Donna stood and lurched forward.

"Changes everything, doesn't it?"

"Yes, Mistress."

"Bounce up and down, do your sexy dance; I want to see how they move."

Joanna's face glowed with pleasure as Donna did her bump and grind, the massive 38DD breasts jiggling and bouncing. "Wonderful! Oh baby, you are gonna be the hit of the party. I expect to see lots of dancing. You are to turn down no one, understand? Anyone asks you to dance and you're to give them your best airhead 'sure!' and go give them their own personal on-the-floor sexy lap dance. Got it?"

"Yes, Mistress."

"Anyone, man or woman, can touch you at anytime, anywhere. It's not a fetish party, but it is adults only and anyone who wants a little piece of you is welcome to it."

"Yes, Mistress."

"OK, let's hide that oversized clitty of yours." Joanna handed Donna a flesh colored gaff. Joanna pulled and stuffed in the chastity device, working it into the smallest package possible and securing it all with fashion tape.

"Now this," said Joanna as she held out a heavy black waist cincher, trimmed in lace, with garter straps, and metal stays, "to give you a pleasing shape," Joanna explained. There were six garters on each leg, because, "Men find lots of garters sexy."

Donna took the black, seamed fishnet stockings and rolled them up her legs. Carefully aligning the seam she fastened each garter.

"Now the dress," Joanna said.

Donna held up her arms and allowed the slinky red cocktail dress to flow down her body. Joanna tugged and pulled here and there, working the tight fabric over her sissy's curves. Using double-sided fashion tape Joanna strategically secured the fabric neatly around the fake breasts. "There," she said, "that will allow maximum visibility and cleavage, but prevent any 'pop-outs'. Remember, if anyone touches these you giggle, swoon, shiver, whatever little sluts who love getting felt up do."

"Yes, Mistress."

"Your shoes are on the bed. Put them on and then let me see you walk and dance."

With a new-found respect for mass and gravity, Donna walked to the bed, the act made more difficult by the skin tight dress and the top-heavy weight of the breasts. Even with the thigh high slit of the dress, walking was difficult.

Donna sat on the edge of the bed and slipped the wicked evening shoes on her stocking-clad feet. Joanna had deliberately chosen a pair designed to attract the male and torment the wearer. They were patent red, with wicked pointed toes and needle-thin five inch stiletto heels. "Walk and do a bit of sexy dancing for me."

Donna thrust out her chest and strutted around the room, the long tight gown helping to keep her steps short and dainty. She put one hand on her hip and the other behind her neck and slinked around the room, the skyscraper heels lending a natural up and down motion to her hips. When she came to an open area she started her bump and grind, running her hands up and down her body, shaking her hair and rotating her hips.

Joanna clapped her hands with glee. "Fan-fucking-tastic! Pure slut! Alex and Brent will be very pleased. Let's get your hair and makeup done and you can spend some time practicing in full costume."

Donna stared at the sexy vixen that gazed back at her from the mirror. Big hair, blonde and teased, fell about her shoulders. Her eyes were dark and smoky, outlined and shadowed in black, with long fluttering eyelashes. The cheekbones were highlighted in blush; her lips, full, sexy and pouting were fuck-me red, matching the wicked stilettos on her feet. The red dress fit like a second skin, clinging to her body, the deep cleavage barely able to contain the mammoth breasts, which due to the backless nature of the dress, were not constrained by a bra. Long, faux-diamond chandelier earrings dropped to her shoulders and caught the light with every move of her head. A matching necklace hung low, a shiny lure to draw attention to the plunging neckline and cleavage. The slit up the slide revealed a hint of stocking top and garters. Shiny spandex gloves came up past her elbow, the cuffs ending in an explosion of red Marabou feathers, more suitable for a stripper then a dinner date. The entire outfit screamed: 'SLUT! FUCK ME!' Donna smiled at the image in the mirror, the voices reassuring her: *I want to be sexy for men. I'm a fuck toy.* She unconsciously began to preen and pose, bend at the waist to expose her cleavage, turn to show the slit and the stocking, and smile at the uber-feminine slut in the mirror who followed her every move.

Joanna shook her head in disbelief. *Karin is a genius. She ought to publish a fucking paper on mind control and behavior modification. This is un-fucking-real.*

"LOOK, BABY, ISN'T SHE PRECIOUS? AND THAT DRESS IS SLIT SO HIGH!"

"YES, SHE'S SURE TO GET A LOT OF ATTENTION TONIGHT, WHETHER SHE WANTS IT OR NOT."

"OH, SHE WANTS IT, DARLING, SHE'S OUR COCK-SUCKING SLUT."

Sixteen

Brent and Alex arrived at seven p.m. When the doorbell rang Donna swished to the door, practicing her walk and learning to find the new balance required between the massive breasts and the spindly stiletto heels. She opened the door and backed away to allow the men in. "Good evening and welcome to Mistress Joanna's house," she said in a sultry and breathy tone.

Alex gazed at the sultry, feminized thing in red standing before him. "So, is this lovely creature my date for this evening?"

With a toss of her blonde tresses Donna slid beside Alex and wrapped a gloved hand around his waist. She coyly rubbed her hip against his and shyly looked up. "That's right, I'm all yours tonight, baby."

Alex, like Brent, was tall and looked down on his date, even in her five inch heels. He turned to

Brent and smiled. "Shit, your friend Joanna is a miracle worker."

Brent nodded his agreement. "If I didn't see I wouldn't believe it myself. Her friend Karin did the initial programming, although Joanna has certainly worked with the basic material to craft a submissive to her exact needs."

Donna ran her gloved hand over Alex's chest, looked up and purred, "Would you like a drink, baby?"

Alex gave her a spank on her ass to send her on her way. "Scotch, neat, for Brent and I."

Donna strutted away without looking back, a hand seductively posed on her hip, shaking her ass as she walked to the bar.

"Shit, Brent, that's unreal. It's really a guy?"

"It's Joanna's husband," Brent replied, "or used to be, still is, I guess, legally. Although around here she's more of a domestic, maid, servant, sex toy. Oh and Joanna would like for you to refer to it as 'her or she.' It helps reinforce the conditioning."

"Yeah, OK, whatever. So I can fuck it, or her?"

"Hey, she's your date, fuck her in the ass, in the mouth, whatever you'd normally do with a date who's a slut."

Alex watched Sissy approach with their drinks on a silver tray. "Well this ought to meet Stearns requirements about male-female couples only at his vanilla soirees. And since he's a bit randy himself maybe I can make a few points with him tonight."

Alex took his drink from the tray and asked

Donna, "Are you ready for this evening?"

Donna excitedly bobbed her head, her long earrings casting reflections of light and color. She blew a kiss at Alex. "Oh yea baby, I'm gonna show you the best time."

Alex smiled and held his glass out for a toast with Brent, "Honey, you may end up showing everyone a good time."

Joanna made her grand entrance down the staircase. Her dark brown hair was pulled up into an elegant chignon, her makeup expertly applied, highlighting her green eyes. An evening gown of beautiful black crepe flowed over her curves, its front cowl neck a teasing prelude to the deep, plunging backless cut of the gown. Satin evening shoes adorned her feet. Unlike Donna, Joanna wore real diamonds on her ears and around her neck. Long black leather gloves seductively snaked up her arms, ending above the elbow. One leather gloved hand held a be-jeweled evening clutch. In direct opposition to Donna's garish, slut look, Joanna was all glamour and elegance, truly beautiful.

Brent walked forward, taking her gloved hand in his and helping her down the last two stairs. "Joanna, you look fabulous."

"Thank you, darling."

Alex stepped forward to embrace Joanna and give her a small kiss. "Yes Joanna, the look is stunning, truly beautiful."

"Thank you so much. And you two gentlemen look ruggedly handsome as well. Alex, what do you think of your date for the evening?"

"Her look is admittedly different than yours, but I have a feeling that both of you will be the centers of attention; although for different reasons. You've done a wonderful job with Donna and I'm very much looking forward to spending the evening with her."

Joanna fixed Donna with a stern look. "She's yours for the evening, Alex, and more, in every sense of the word. She's been instructed not to disappoint you. Do what you want with her, and let me know if there are any problems. Will there be any problems?"

Donna rubbed up against Alex, pulling his arm behind her and placing his hand on her writhing ass. "Oh no, Mistress, there won't be any problems. I'll be the perfect date for Master Alex. I will, I promise." As she finished speaking Donna rubbed her gloved hand over Alex's chest.

Alex shook his head, smiled, looked at Joanna and mouthed the words, 'Thank you.'

Brent drove the two couples to the dinner party. Alex, in gentlemanly fashion, held the door open for Donna, who demurely slid into the seat. When Alex took his seat she cuddled up next to him, allowing him to put his arm around her.

Joanna observed it all in the vanity mirror.

"Very sweet, keep it up, an obedient slut will be rewarded, bad behavior will be punished."

Donna snuggled closer to Alex and nuzzled his ear. "I'll be very good, Mistress."

Brent laughed and shook his head. "Joanna you are one cruel and manipulating bitch."

Joanna finished checking her makeup in the vanity mirror and flipped up the visor, "Some of my better qualities, darling."

Patrick Stearns was a man of wealth, power and privilege and his mansion reflected such. A long winding private drive took them off the main road and to the gates of the Stearns compound. A guard at the gate checked them off the guest list and directed them to guest parking. Alex gave the keys to one valet as another opened the doors for the ladies in the car. Joanna and Donna exited, smoothed their dresses and took their escort's arms.

Donna was wide eyed as Alex led her up the granite steps to the spacious entrance. A liveried doorman opened the door and they entered the foyer where a butler ushered them to the grand ballroom. She unconsciously edged closer to Alex, feeling his arm firmly around her waist. "Your boss lives large, this is awesome."

Alex bent down to nibble on her ear, "Yea,

he's rich and likes to show it. And while he puts on this pompous attitude of family values and traditional marriage he's a fucking pervert with a dungeon in the basement. He loves to work over his own little stable of girls and boys."

Donna reached up to plant a kiss on his cheek and wipe off the lipstick smudge with her glove. "And you know this how, baby?"

"A few select people in the scene know about him, but he's so powerful that he'll literally destroy anyone who might attempt to expose him."

The group entered the ballroom, stopping to accept Champagne from a perfectly turned out maid in black dress, white apron and lace headpiece.

Donna gave the maid more than a passing look. *I have an identical outfit at home; I could just as easily be serving drinks here.*

Joanna lightly touched Donna's arm, "Go and fix your makeup."

Standing on the tip toes of her high heels Donna gave Alex a little kiss. "I'm going to fix my makeup baby; I'll be right back."

As she left Alex patted her ass and she turned to give him a big smile.

Alex watched his date walk away, the red heels clicking on the marble floor and the slit in the dress exposing the occasional stocking top. He turned to Joanna, "I can't believe that's your husband."

"I suppose he's, she's not, not anymore. But she's very useful as a maid and plaything. I think you'll enjoy her tonight."

"Yes, I do intend to enjoy her. She's the perfect slut."

Joanna sipped her Champagne, the glistening crystal glass blazing against her black leather glove. "Yes, well this evening is the product of extensive training and the fear of failure and the resulting punishment. Make sure you get her on the dance floor tonight. I'm sure that you and everyone else will be quite entertained."

Donna garnered several looks from both men and women as she sashayed to the ladies room. Her bright red dress, gloves and shoes stood out, an obvious premeditated ploy of Joanna's. The women derisively said, "She's a slut!" while the men gleefully said, "She's a slut!"

In the ladies room Donna sat at the vanity and freshened her makeup, applying more eyeliner and mascara and touching up her lipstick. There were several bottles of expensive perfume on the vanity and she sprayed perfume up and down her cleavage. The woman to her right gave her a disdainful look, but Donna simply smiled, lifted her dress and gave herself another spray between the legs, "He just loves it when I smell pretty down there." Donna rose and left the room; the seated woman's face a portrait of shock and disgust.

When Donna rejoined the group they had collected another couple. Alex made the introductions. "Steve, this is my date for the night, Donna."

Steve was in his mid-50s, average height and a bit overweight. His wife was a reed thin woman with a black cocktail dress that seemed to hang from her. He leaned over to give Donna a kiss. "Donna, huh? This is my wife, Gloria. I work with Alex in Acquisitions."

Hooking her arm in Alex's Donna addressed the new couple. "I'm so pleased to meet you both. Alex never tells me much about his work."

"Well little lady, Alex hasn't mentioned you either. We're rather surprised to see Alex here with you; we didn't know he was involved with anyone."

Donna ran her fingers up Alex's chest and tickled his chin. "Well, we are involved, aren't we baby?"

Alex cupped her ass with his hand and pulled her closer to him, bending down to kiss her. "Yes, we certainly are involved. Would you like to meet some of the others?"

She almost squeaked as she replied, "Sure!"

Across the room Patrick Stearns sipped his Champagne, made polite small talk and studied the blonde in the red dress and gloves. While everyone else at the party was dressed in subtle, cocktail style, this creature blazed like a beacon. Obviously she wasn't the most beautiful woman in the room. She certainly didn't possess the classic beauty of the stunning brunette with Brent. But still there was something provocative about her: that skintight, low-cut, high-slit dress, those long Marabou-trimmed gloves and the fuck-me heels screamed SEX! And Patrick Stearns was not the person to miss those kinds of signs. "Excuse me, please," he said as he made his way across the room, stopping occasionally to shake hands or complement a woman's dress.

With an air of absolute authority he made his way to Alex. "Brent, Alex, so glad you could make it this evening." Turning to Joanna he extended a hand. "You must be Joanna. Your beauty exceeds that of your picture on Brent's desk."

Donna shrank back a bit, but managed to keep the party smile on her face. *My wife, my Mistress's picture is on Brent's desk at work?* Then came the voice: **Mistress must be allowed all pleasures. I will serve Mistress and her lovers.**

After the usual glad-handing and polite small talk Stearns turned to Alex. "Please do introduce me to this ravishing beauty you've brought tonight. Been hiding her away have you?" Stearns reached out to take Donna's hand. "I'm Patrick Stearns, your host for this evening and I'm delighted you're here. And you are?"

Donna smiled and bent forward, thrusting her plunging cleavage into view. Holding out a gloved hand she squeaked, "I'm Sissy Donna."

"Really?" Stearns smiled. "Indeed you are. And are you having a good time, Donna, being a good girl, are you?" he asked with a sly wink.

Donna wiggled her bottom and bosom in reply, surprising Joanna, *where did she learn that?*

"Oh yes, the party is fantastic. And of course I'm being a good girl," she replied as she rubbed her hips against Alex. She stood on tiptoe to give Alex a kiss. "If I was a bad girl I'd get spanked, wouldn't I, baby?" Donna turned back to Stearns, batting her long eyelashes, "Your house is so beautiful Mr. Stearns."

Stearns' eyes lit up and a cruel smile played across his lips. "I'd love to show you around later, give you a peek at some of the special rooms."

Donna literally bounced up and down, her large breasts making the red fabric of the dress flow like lava. She looked imploringly at Alex. "Oh can we baby, can Mr. Stearns show me the special rooms later, please honey?"

Alex shrugged his shoulders and smiled at Stearns. "How can I say no?"

"Indeed," Stearns agreed. He plucked a glass of Champagne from a passing waiter and handed it to Donna. "We must see that this lovely creature is very well taken care of. I promise you my dear, an evening you won't soon forget."

Before they adjourned to the dining room for dinner Joanna suggested the 'girls' go to the powder room.

"You're doing very well," offered Joanna as she touched up her blush. "Alex is enjoying himself and his boss, Mr. Stearns seems quite taken with you as well."

"Thank you, Mistress, I'm trying very hard." Donna added more lipstick.

"It seems they believe you are female, albeit a rather cheap and slutty one. But you may be able to make that work for you."

"Yes, Mistress, I understand."

"Do whatever you have to do to get through the evening and keep all these men happy. Anything, understand?"

After dinner everyone assembled in the Grand Salon for a concert by a well known jazz pianist. Patrick Stearns made the rounds before the concert, seeing to the comfort of his guests. He made his way to Alex and Donna as the pianist launched into his first number. "Would you like to stay and listen, or perhaps have a tour of the house?"

Donna smiled at Stearns, "I'd love a tour. Can we, baby?" she asked.

Alex smiled and extended his hand, indicating to Stearns to lead the way.

Stearns offered his arm and Donna linked her gloved arm in his. They walked down the hallway, their host occasionally stopping to offer a short commentary on a particular painting or vase, the details lost on Donna, who simply squealed with delight and wiggled up against Stearns.

As they turned left to enter another corridor Stearns nodded to a tall, austere butler at the end of the hall. The somber butler with the high fore-head gave a short bow and disappeared behind a door.

The sounds of the piano music now long distant, the three stopped and Stearns turned to Donna. "So you're spanked when you've been a bad girl?"

Donna bit her lip and cocked her head, her right toe coming off the floor and her foot waving seductively on the rapier-thin stiletto heel. "Uh-huh. Oh, I try not to be bad; I try to be a good girl, but sometimes I fuck up. Oh! I meant, sometimes I'm not good."

Stearns laughed and stroked her cheek. "It's OK, baby, you can say 'fuck'. Sometimes I have to spank my girls as well; it's hard for you to be good all the time. Would you like to see where I punish bad girls?"

Donna put her finger in her mouth, silently sucked on it and nodded her head.

Stearns wrapped his arm around her and slipped his hand down to cup her ass as he led her and Alex through a door and down a flight of stairs. The stairwell was richly appointed with thick carpet and wood paneled walls. The walls displayed a wide array of erotic oil paintings and photographs that would find a home in any museum of erotic art. At the bottom of the stairs they entered a foyer with a small wet bar, leather chairs and elegant lighting. Past this warm and inviting space was a large expanse of blackness.

"In there," pointed Stearns, "is where bad

girls get punished. Do you want to go in?"

Donna turned to Alex who stood behind her and Stearns. "Can we, baby, I'd really like to see it."

"I'd be very interested as well," Alex said.

Stearns flipped a switch, the darkness receded and his dungeon was revealed. The walls were rough-hewn stone and the floor a smooth and polished concrete. Throughout the room faux candles flickered in medieval looking iron sconces. Cleverly hidden in the massive wooden ceiling beams were spotlights that illuminated each piece of equipment. And what an array of equipment populated the dungeon: an iron cage, a St. Andrews cross, a spanking bench, bondage table, a pillory, stocks and several futuristic pieces that neither Alex nor Donna could identify. Throughout the room were assortments of canes, whips, floggers, crops, manacles, hoods, gags and every piece of bondage equipment one could imagine.

"Very impressive, very," Alex said.

Stearns responded with a slight bow. "Thank you. Before you go in, my dear, you must be collared."

From the far side of the dungeon the tall butler appeared, his coat removed but the elegant shirt, vest and tie still in place. He walked to the group and stopped before Donna, a leather collar in his hand.

With a look of expectation to both Alex and Stearns, Donna stepped forward and raised her chin, elongating her neck, allowing the butler to quickly and expertly affix the collar.

Stearns nodded to the butler. "This is Simmons, indispensable in the dungeon. He is a man of many talents. Simmons, our guests tonight are Alex and his date Sissy Donna."

Simmons ignored Donna, but gave a curt bow to Alex. "Welcome to The Stearns Dungeon, sir, very pleased to make your acquaintance."

Alex nodded in return, "Likewise."

Stearns clipped a short leather lead to a D-ring on Donna's collar. "Now that our little bitch is properly attired, let me show you around." With a pull he stepped forward, leading them into the dungeon.

Seventeen

Donna's heels echoed in the harsh stillness as she followed Stearns through a tour of his dungeon. Their journey ended at the spanking horse. With a tug on her leash he pulled Donna forward, delighting in how her tits jiggled on the precarious heels. "Well my dear, care to give it a try?"

"But I've been good tonight, haven't I?" she implored.

Stearns cruelly laughed and jerked the leash, pulling her face-to-face with him. "Being well behaved has nothing to do with it, but we'll see how good you can be, unless Alex here wants to put a stop to it."

"It could make for an entertaining evening," Alex answered.

Stearns reached out to shake Alex's hand. "Agreed, a quick romp and we rejoin the party."

Before releasing Alex's hand Stearns looked him in the eye. "But you must promise to bring her back, for a more extended visit."

Alex flashed his most evil and conspiratorial smile, "Love to."

Stearns grabbed Donna by the hair, pulled her head back and cruelly brought his mouth down on hers. His tongue drove into her mouth, not a kiss of passion; it was a kiss of domination. Just as violently he broke the kiss. "Simmons! Tie this slut down."

Simmons placed his hand on Donna's back and pushed her face down, over the horse. A wide leather strap went across her back, securing her middle to the leather padded spanking horse. He moved behind her and pulled up her dress, exposing her garter belt, seamed stockings and red lace panties.

Stearns licked his lips and stepped forward, slapping Donna's ass with his meaty hand, smiling as he watched the reddened hand print bloom on her ass. "A lovely picture." He spread her ass cheeks apart his fingers probing and searching when he suddenly stopped and looked up in surprise. "Alex, it seems you've brought us a girl with a little something extra. Excellent!" His hand grabbed the tight package concealing Donna's cock and balls, squeezing and pulling. "A shemale slut; are the tits real?"

"Unfortunately not," Alex said.

Stearns squeezed harder on the balls, eliciting a wail from Donna.

Again Stearn's massive hand reddened the taut ass before him. "Shut up, girl!" He turned to Alex. "We could give her real tits if you'd like. I know some doctors who have a unique practice: big tits, hideous nipples, whatever you want."

"Yes," mused Alex, "it is intriguing. But she doesn't belong to me; she's Joanna's sissy maid husband."

"Really? I say Alex, you keep very interesting company. Yes, you're quite right, property and all that, I'll speak to Joanna. I'm sure I could arrange a surgical procedure in return for services-in-kind."

Simmons pulled Donna's legs apart and fastened each ankle to the outer legs of the horse.

"No gag," Stearns ordered. "I want to hear her cries and moans."

Simmons moved in front of her and locked down her wrists in the same manner.

Alex and Stearns circled the hapless sissy. She was, indeed, quite a sight: tied face down over the spanking horse, arms and legs spread and tethered and her dress pulled up around her waist.

Stearns nodded approvingly. "Warm her up Simmons, the elk-hide flogger, I think." Turning to Alex he whispered, "Watch this, Simmons is an artist."

Simmons clicked his heels in a menacing, Prussian fashion and began with firm strokes to her ass and thighs.

Donna fell into the rhythm of the blows,

moaning with pleasure, enjoying the caress of the leather until Simmons brought a hard strike up from the bottom, right between her legs. She yelped and lurched forward as much as her restraints would allow.

Simmons continued; the blows now delivered with more force. He put a snap in them, stinging her with the leather tails. When she raised her head she saw Alex and Stearns watching her, their faces a mixture of pleasure and excitement.

Stearns locked his eyes on hers, reached over and selected a thin rattan cane from an antique umbrella stand filled with canes and crops. He menacingly flexed the cane and violently sliced the air with it, the wicked reed making a harrowing sound as it cut the air. Donna's eyes showed fear.

"Good, you should be afraid," Stearns teased as he walked behind her. He tapped the cane on her bottom, amused as she flinched and bounced at each blow.

Donna watched Alex move in front of her. He unzipped his pants, his hands pulling away the fly of his trousers to remove his meaty cock.

He stepped forward, and slapped her in the face with his growing organ. "You're going to let our host enjoy his pleasures with the cane. But keep in mind what you'll have in your mouth. If you lose control and bite down I'll let him flay the skin off that pretty little ass."

Donna's opened her mouth to greet the bulbous head of his cock with her tongue.

The first blow of the cane fell across the middle of her buttocks. The initial sensation was the strike of the rattan on the flesh itself. Then came the deeper bloom of pain within the muscle, a pain that grew in intensity only to be interrupted by the second stroke.

This wasn't the first time that she'd had been caned. Mistress Karin introduced Joanna to the cane and both women had put Donna through her paces in such discipline. But Stearns wielded it as if it was an extension of his being. She felt the power, the malice in each stroke.

The next blow, and the next, landed in that oh-so-sweet and tender spot between the bottom of the buttocks and the top of the thighs.

Her ability to focus and endure the pain afflicting her ass were challenged by the cock that invaded her mouth. Alex grabbed her head and pulled himself into her.

His hips thrust forward. "Take it, deeper, take it!" He slowly pulled her down on his swollen shaft as he counted, "10-9-8-7-6-5-4-3-2-out!" He pulled her mouth from his cock as she gagged and gasped for air. Just as she thought she'd found relief she felt the savage cane bite into her ass and she screeched as Alex growled, "Again," and pulled her mouth back down.

She wiggled her ass in a futile attempt to avoid the blows and cool the pain of fire that infested her bottom.

Stearns' large and meaty hand pinched and slapped at the red welts that striped her ass. He snapped her garter strap and laughed as she flinched. "The slapper, Simmons."

Simmons quickly produced the leather slapper and handed it to his employer.

Stearns used the slapper and painted wide red stripes over the thin cruel welts of the cane. "She's going to look quite lovely tomorrow. And I doubt she'll be sitting much."

Alex pulled Donna's lips from his cock, a thin drool of saliva and pre-cum linking his massive cock and her wet open mouth. He looked down at her, pleased to see her mouth open, yearning, her tongue reaching out for the cock she now so desperately wanted. "Shit, this slut loves to have a cock in her mouth. Don't you, huh?" he said, holding his engorged member in one hand and slapping her in the face with it. "You want this big cock in your mouth?"

"Yes, baby, yes!" she screamed.

"You ought to get some of this" Alex said as he shoved his cock back into her mouth. "Try out this mouth."

"I believe I will," Stearns said as he handed the slapper to Simmons.

Alex pulled out, pleased with the way that Donna desperately moaned at being denied his massive cock. He would definitely send Joanna a beautiful flower arrangement tomorrow. Her husband, Donna, was a great date. He glanced at Simmons, "Lubricant?"

As if by magic Simmons produced a tube of lubricant. Alex moved behind Donna, uncapped the lid, placed the tube in her ass and squeezed. He laughed as she gasped. He inserted one finger, then two, and watched her moan and relax into the horse.

As Alex probed her asshole Stearns dropped his pants to expose a shorter than average but very thick cock. He rubbed his cock around her lips and, just as Alex had, found the same inviting tongue flicking out to welcome and taste his manhood. "Flick your tongue over the tip, quickly and lightly, that's the way I like it."

She complied, her tongue, cat-like, making love to Stearn's cock.

Alex pulled his fingers from the gaping sissy pussy and looked disgustedly at mess on his fingers. He grabbed Donna's hair and wiped his hands, leaving a sticky residue in matted clumps of hair.

Stearns watched and nodded his approval at this further debasement of their prize. "Alex, you must return for one of my private parties and bring this lovely fuck slut with you!" He punctuated the last word by driving his short fat cock as deeply as he could into her mouth.

The huge fleshy intruder stretched her mouth even more than Alex's cock and she feared she would dislocate her jaw. She was lost now, consumed in a world of submission to The Cock. As Stearns grabbed the back of her head and pumped her face up and down on his cock Alex invaded her from the rear. Her resistance to this back door entry was mercifully minimal. Joanna had trained her ass with various butt plugs and Alex's cock made only a moment's hesitation before sliding in. That brief bit of discomfort was replaced by the warm fullness of being filled. In her sexual delirium she hoped that both cocks might meet within her core, their spewing seed consuming her. She bucked wildly on the horse, but restrained she found little freedom of movement.

As if it was a voice from another world she heard Alex growl, "Here it comes, slut!" She felt him stiffen and lurch and she clenched her buttocks to milk every bit of his precious man-seed into her sissy pussy.

Stearns exploded in her mouth, filling it with powerful spurts of creamy cum. Quickly he pulled out, put his hand under her chin and closed her mouth. He slapped her face, hard. "Don't swallow! Hold it in there."

Alex slid his well-used cock from Donna's ass, grabbed a handful of her hair, and once again wiped himself clean.

Both men stood before her as she looked up at them, her eyes glazed, her mouth closed and her cheeks bulging with loads of cum.

Simmons took several pictures with a digital camera. "You don't mind, do you?" asked Stearns.

"Not at all," smiled Alex. "I'd like copies."

Stearns slapped Alex on the back, "Of course, of course." He turned to Donna, fixing her with a lecherous glare. "Open!"

She opened her mouth, strands of cum and

drool connecting her top and bottom lips, her tongue buried in a reservoir of pooling, glistening, pearly-white cum. Her eyes blinked at the camera flash as Simmons moved in to take close-ups of her face and cum-filled mouth.

"A very pretty picture," Stearns said. "I'll have Simmons do a Photoshop eight by ten for your desk at work. He's quite skilled, both in the dungeon and at the computer."

Donna recoiled in horror at the humiliation of such a public display.

"Thank you, that's very generous," Alex replied.

Simmons continued to shoot pictures from every angle as Stearns bent down to look Donna in the eyes. "Gargle!" he commanded.

Eyes wide with fear and face burning with shame, she allowed some of the horrid cum to slide down her throat and gargled. Simmons switched the camera to movie mode to catch the action. Alex and Stearns chuckled at the way the cum bubbled off her tongue.

"Swallow - slowly, savor the taste and the texture," Stearns ordered. "Show us how much you need it."

She gulped and slowly swallowed the men's seed. When her mouth was empty she licked her lips, seeking out and lapping up every drop of the precious spunk.

The men laughed, enjoying the spectacle of total submission, humiliation and degradation.

"Let's adjourn to the foyer and relax with a

Cognac and a cigar," Stearns offered. He turned to Donna, now swallowing the last dregs of cum. "Did you enjoy yourself, my little slut?"

Nodding in the affirmative, she whispered, "Simmons."

"Simmons?" Stearns asked.

Donna's eyes imploringly sought Simmons. "His cock - please?"

Alex and Stearns roared with laughter. "Well done! Bravo! She's a true slut, two cocks in her mouth and one in her ass and she wants more," Stearns exclaimed. "Yes, my dear, you shall have more. Simmons, you may serve our Cognac and cigars while we relax in the sitting area and then you can come back here and finish this slut. Come Alex, you and I can talk and watch your date's last act for the evening as we relax."

Simmons prepared Cognac and cigars as Alex and Stearns seated themselves in comfortable wing back chairs facing the dungeon. Drinks and cigars in hand they watched Simmons stride purposefully back to the dungeon area and take his place in front of Donna.

Stearns swirled the amber colored liquor in his glass, lifting it to his nose to catch the bouquet. He inhaled the fragrance and then took the liquid into his mouth. For a moment he let it play on his tongue, finally swallowing and nodding his approval, "Quite excellent." He turned to Alex, "Funny you never came up on my radar before, but now that you have I see big things for you."

Alex held up his own glass in salute, nodded

his thanks, and puffed on his cigar. "I've certainly enjoyed this evening."

In the dungeon Simmons was thrusting his cock deep into Donna's mouth. Across the room the men could hear her moaning and the sound of Simmon's rather large balls slapping her chin.

"Enjoys his work, does he?" Alex asked.

"He's very useful, in any number of ways, and quite well endowed. Yes Alex, you've made quite an impression on me tonight. Of course your work has always been excellent, first-rate. But I'd always imagined you different somehow; and tonight I find you are, but in a way very much in accord with my own differences."

Simmons was now into a rhythm: thrusting and holding, easing back and thrusting again.

"I enjoy my work - and my leisure activities," Alex said.

"Yes, I see that now. I'm giving you the Harrison account." Stearns reached over to shake Alex's hand. "I know you'll do the company proud. I'll be seeing more of you, at work and expect to see you and that lovely little slut at my more exclusive gatherings."

"Thank you, I won't let you down. And my - our," Alex said nodding at Donna, "calendar will always be open."

Stearns offered up his glass for a toast, "Most excellent!"

"Sir," Simmons grunted, close to his peak, "shall I come in her ass or her mouth?"

"The mouth; we need to get back to the party."

Simmons held her head tight to his crotch and growled. "Take it all, but don't swallow." He threw back his head, moaned and shot thick streams of cum into her mouth.

Donna tried to hold it, but there was too much and his cock was too big. Some of the precious fluid slipped down her throat and she gagged, tasting the milky white fluid and hearing the voice: *Men like it when I gag and swallow, I love to suck cock.*

When he pulled out, Simmons wiped his cock on her face, noting that her eyes were still locked on him. "Open," he ordered.

She opened, revealing, for the second time that evening, a mouthful of drool and cum. Simmons smiled with satisfaction. "The Master will be pleased." He held out a small jar, popped off the lid and dropped a cherry in her mouth. He bent low and whispered in her ear. "When I release the bonds, you will get down on your hands and knees and crawl across the room to Master and his guest. You will keep your mouth open and show them your treat. Do you understand?"

Donna nodded and waited while Simmons removed her restraints. She hadn't realized how stiff and sore she'd become from the ordeal and Simmons had to help her off the horse and onto the floor. She crawled across the room, her mouth open and her eyes fixed on her two Masters. The polished concrete floor was cool on her hands and knees, the sensation providing a brief respite from the degradation she'd suffered. As she approached the men she dipped her back and tried to elongate her spine, seeking to give herself a lean and sultry look. She stopped before Stearns and offered herself, thrusting her opened mouth forward.

Stearns smiled and motioned Alex over. When Alex bent to look he saw Donna's lips parted, her mouth a pool of cum with a red cherry floating on the top.

"Simmons gave her a treat, one of his specialties, a cum sundae," Stearns boasted. He patted Donna on the head, as one would a beloved pet. "Do you like your treat?"

She nodded her head and batted her cum-stained eyelashes, never taking her eyes of adoration off Stearns. At that moment she never wanted to be anywhere but at the feet of these men.

Stearns smiled and melted her heart. "You may swallow," he said.

Donna slowly let Simmons' seed slide down her throat, seductively chewing the cherry and licking her lips as she finished.

"There's a door behind you, the lady's room." Stearns pointed to a door behind Donna. "You will crawl in there and clean yourself up. You'll find what you need. You're not the first slut that needed to fix herself up to rejoin a party."

Without being told, and without knowing why, Donna bent forward to plant kisses of obeisance on the shoes of Alex and Stearns. With her eyes on the floor she silently backed away, turned and crawled to the bathroom.

Stearns turned to Alex and flashed a broad smile. "She's a keeper Alex."

Donna was unsteady and glassy-eyed when they finally rejoined the party. In the bathroom she'd fixed her hair and makeup as best she could and straightened her clothing. Her mouth and ass ached after being stretched by a continual succession of real-man-cocks, and her own sissy clitty was throbbing fruitlessly in its restraints. The experience had been humiliating and degrading, but it excited her and something in her wanted to get back to the dungeon as soon as possible.

My pleasure comes from giving pleasure. I am a fuck toy.

Joanna's eyes met Alex's and she smiled evilly as Donna teetered forward in her heels. "Did everyone have a good time?"

Alex and Stearns said, "We did."

Joanna turned to Donna and teased, "And did Donna have a good time?"

"Yes, Mistress."

Stearns gave Donna a spank on her bottom. "When we finished with her she begged for the butler!"

Joanna's eyes opened wide in mock surprise. "Really? What did you do?"

There was no further shame that could be endured that evening and Donna readily replied, "I sucked his cock, it was wonderful, he gave me a cum sundae!"

"Did you, really?" Joanna replied with delight and pride.

Stearns addressed the group, now including his wife Caroline, who'd joined them. "I'm giving the Harrison account to Alex," he announced.

There, ensued all-around congratulations and shaking of hands.

Caroline gave Donna a long look. "Did I hear you say you gave my butler a blow job?"

"Uh, yes Ma'am," replied a hesitant Donna, now worried that she'd committed a breach of party protocol.

"Is there a problem?" Joanna asked.

"Not at all," said Caroline, "I'm impressed, Simmons is rather well-endowed."

"You know this of your butler?" asked a surprised Joanna.

"Yes, as my butler he performs many personal services." She turned to her husband. "So tell me, darling was she fun?"

Stearns put his arm around his wife and kissed her. "A marvelous piece of work. I've invited Alex, and her, back for a party."

Caroline made a sweeping gesture to the group. "I do hope you'll all attend. I'm sure we'd all love to play with this delicate little creature."

"MISTRESS SAYS I'M GOING TO BE INVITED TO MORE PARTIES! I CAN'T WAIT. SHE SAID I WAS GOING TO FUCK LIKE A RABBIT SO I HOPE THIS COSTUME IS OK. I WANT TO BE SEXY AND PRETTY FOR ALL THE MISTRESSES AND MASTERS. THEY LIKE TO PLAY WITH SISSY SLUTS AND MASTER SAYS I'M A REAL PARTY GIRL AND WILL BE VERY POPULAR."

Eighteen

Monday morning came early for Donna and the weekend had been anything but relaxing. Still there were duties to perform: run Mistress Joanna's bath, help Mistress dress, and prepare and serve breakfast. She fluffed out her petticoats, straightened the white lacy headpiece and minced into Mistress's bedroom.

Joanna sat at her dressing table putting on earrings. "The black patent pumps," she ordered.

Donna curtsied and teetered over to the closet to retrieve Mistress's shoes. She returned and knelt to hold the shoes as Joanna slid her feet into each stylish pump.

With a casual wave of the hand Joanna dismissed her sissified husband/maid. "Make my coffee to go, I'm late. I'll e-mail you your tasks for the day. Until then you can have free time."

Those were the last words Donna heard from Mistress that morning. Joanna breezed through the kitchen grabbing her purse, briefcase and coffee, and leaving without another word.

Donna looked at the clock. She'd have forty-five minutes before Joanna e-mailed an impossible-to-complete list of chores for the day. *Free time, what a misnomer.* There was no freedom for her in this house, no physical or mental freedom, no escape from the restraints of submission and slavery. *A slave, that's really what I am.*

She knelt before the computer in Joanna's home office. Unless given specific permission, she wasn't allowed to sit on the furniture. So she sat on the floor and idly thumbed through a popular women's magazine, male-subject magazines weren't on her allowed reading list; *free time, to do what?* The television was locked out with a code and Joanna used a software program to track unauthorized computer use. Donna could access the computer only for work-related uses: recipes, makeup and housekeeping tips, and special tasks for Mistress.

Still it was good to have a few moments of peace and quiet. She sipped her weight-loss shake, *Mistress thinks I need to lose a few more pounds*, and thought about the past weekend.

They'd stayed at the Stearns' party for an hour after her session in the dungeon. Ever the dutiful date, she'd hung on Alex's arm, giggled and planted sweet butterfly kisses on his cheek.

Joanna beamed at the uber-feminine display by her husband. Was it his fear of her displeasure or the conditioning of Karin's cage that was driving him to such attempts to be a feminized public slut? In the end she decided it didn't matter, although she hoped that he was afraid of not meeting her standards. If he was operating strictly on conditioning he wouldn't feel the shame and embarrassment of being a date in drag for a Gay man. And she wanted him to always know what he was: a sissy husband, a maid, a fuck-toy, HER property.

Brent pulled Joanna close as they watched Donna and Alex dance. Donna shook and undulated, rubbing her body against an enthusiastic Alex. Joanna raised her Champagne glass in a mock toast to her sissy. "She's giving it her all; I'll admit that."

Brent nuzzled her neck and whispered in her ear, "Yes, we seem to have pulled off our deception this evening. Alex said that Stearns was quite taken with your sexy she-male, evidently they're quite the popular commodity at his dungeon parties. Stearns wants Alex and his sissy slut back for another session."

"I'll admit I'd like to attend one of those parties. Give me a cigarette, darling. It's wonderful that Alex got the big account, our Donna was quite the successful slut tonight."

"You two look like you're enjoying yourselves," Joanna said, when Alex and Donna joined them at the table.

Donna nodded enthusiastically, "Oh yes, Mistress."

"It's been a great evening. I couldn't ask for a better date." Alex kissed Donna's hand. "I'd like to take her home. I'll bring her back Sunday evening."

The shock was evident on Donna's face. *Am I going to be pimped out the entire weekend? I've been so good, done what I was told, sucked three cocks and got ass fucked. I just want to go home.*

Joanna witnessed the change. *His hopes are crushed, he's going to be someone's bitch all weekend, despair, how precious.* "Of course, Alex, Brent and I can get along fine on our own. Donna can catch up on her chores next week. She has a small overnight bag in the trunk. Go along girl, do what you're told. You've been very good tonight. If Alex gives you a good report after the weekend I will let you play with yourself for - ten minutes."

In the recesses of her mind Donna heard the voice, *I must obey Mistress. I must please men.* "Yes, Mistress, thank you, Mistress."

Joanna stroked Donna's cheek, "Such a good girl. You run along and be a good date for Alex, show him a good time."

Alex smiled and slipped his hand on Donna's

thigh. "She's already shown me quite a good time, Joanna! But I'm sure we'll get along just fine."

Brent dropped Alex and Donna off at Alex's apartment. Alex carried her overnight bag and escorted Donna to the bedroom. "Why don't you change into something sexy and I'll get us a drink."

Left alone in the room Donna opened the small bag. Joanna had this well planned; all there was for nighttime wear was a sheer black teddy and black high-heeled mules. She undressed, placed her evening gown on a hanger and slipped into the black nightgown and heels. She touched up her makeup and liberally sprayed herself with perfume. *Men like me to smell sexy.* She had no solvent to remove the breast forms so they had to stay on until – until Joanna decided to remove them. Her final act was to smooth the sheer fabric over her body, then go to her lover.

Alex gave her an appreciative look as she did a full turn, putting her assets on display. "Very nice," he said, handing her a glass of white wine. He took a seat, beckoning her to sit on his lap.

Men like it when I walk sexy. She slinked to Alex, taking small steps and crossing her legs with each step. She demurely settled on his lap as he put his arm around her waist.

"You put on quite a show tonight."

She ran her hand through his hair and licked her lips. "I'm glad I could help, baby."

"Did you like having strange cocks in your mouth?"

Men like it when I suck their cocks. I like it, too. "Yes, I did. They were so big, they filled my mouth, but I liked it."

Alex pulled her down, his mouth meeting hers in a cruel kiss. Donna melted into his embrace, forgetting that they were both men, not caring she'd never been alone with a man before. As her cock began to swell in its chastity device she felt the physical pains of frustration and winced.

Alex broke the kiss. "What's wrong, baby?"

She nodded to the space between her legs. "It hurts."

He kissed her again. "I can't fix that, Joanna didn't give me the key." He smiled, "Are you horny?"

"Oh god, baby, yes," she clung to him.

He playfully flicked at her ass. "Best I can do to satisfy you is to take care of this."

Serpent-like, she uncoiled from his embrace and slid from his grasp, sliding to the floor with her head resting between his legs. She pulled out his cock, looked up and smiled, batting her long eyelashes. "I want this in my ass, please, baby, fuck me bad." *Men like it when I beg to be fucked.*

Alex let his head fall back as she took his shaft in his mouth. "Yea, I'm gonna fuck you good."

Joanna smiled as she hit SEND and condemned her sissy maid to another day of drudgery. *Keeps her occupied and out of trouble. And my life is now one of complete luxury and indulgence. Who knew that a few sex games could lead to this?* But it had, and now she had the best of both worlds, a handsome Alpha male in her bed as a lover and a submissive sissy husband seeing to her every need, whim and comfort. *Woman of leisure, spoiled bitch? I can live with either of those.*

"Miss Calloway on line one," came the singsong voice of her personal assistant, Pam.

"Karin, how good to hear from you; how was Las Vegas?"

"Oppressively hot, but who goes outside except for tourists with fanny packs and cameras."

"I can picture it now," Joanna laughed. "But the shopping…"

"Yes, well there's always shopping, isn't there?"

"And you left your little Suzette with Sheila?"

"Oh yes, she doesn't mind a bit of babysitting and she works his ass off. She is rather strict. So what about you? How did Donna do on her first date? I can't wait to hear all the juicy details. Are there pictures, video?"

"Yes, Alex said that the Butler was taking some pictures in the dungeon."

"The dungeon!" Karin shrieked, "and the Butler? Give darling, details please!"

"Well, I only got it second hand, from Alex, but according to him..." Joanna relayed the events at the Stearns party to Karin, who listened attentively, asking few questions.

"It sounds like the conditioning is taking," Karin replied. "From the way you tell it, there wasn't any resistance at all."

"There seemed to be moments, a slight bit of hesitation sometimes, and then he snaps out of it and goes ahead. It's like he's waiting - for something."

Karin chuckled over the phone. "He's hearing the voices. When he's confronted by something that he wouldn't normally do, say suck a cock or date a Gay man he needs to wait for that affirmation to arise from his subconscious: 'I like to suck cock.' And then everything's OK."

"Makes sense."

"With more time in the Breaking Cage we could remove his hesitation and doubt."

"No," replied Joanna. "I'm good with what we have now. I don't want him totally brainwashed. He needs to realize what he is, a submissive sissy husband who does whatever he's told, whether or not it's part of his basic nature. I like that bit of initial fear and loathing when he has to commit those acts, and then that look of resignation and humiliation as he submits."

"You've got a point. It's always best to let them have a memory of where they came from so they know how far they've fallen; exactly where they are."

Donna finished her weight-loss drink and closed up the magazine. The weekend was over. Alex had used her every way she could possibly be used and dropped her off Sunday evening. True to her word Joanna let her play with herself and it didn't take the entire ten minutes to get herself off. Everyone had been pleased with her performance, even Donna herself. Even now she missed the feeling of Alex's cock in her mouth and ass. *It's good to be a fuck toy.*

The computer screen flickered as Joanna's message downloaded. Donna hit the print button and the machine printed out a list of tasks that would take the rest of the day. She pulled the paper from the tray, yet all she could think about was Alex's cock. *It's good to be a fuck toy.*

"MISTRESS SAYS SISSY SLUTS NEED TO DRESS SEXY AND PRACTICE SEXY POSES IF THEY WANT TO GET MORE COCK. I HOPE MASTER LIKES MY NEW BRA AND PANTY SET. THIS IS MY POSE TO GET HIM ALL EXCITED 'CAUSE I CAN'T WAIT TO HAVE HIM DO ME AGAIN. OHH, THAT COCK......"

Nineteen

"*A swinging party*, wife swapping?" Joanna asked.

"Most are married, there are some unmarried couples and the odd single or two; but yea, that's basically it, lots of sex, swapping partners," Brent replied.

"And this is with...?" Joanna held out her wine glass.

"Paul Martin and his wife, you met them at Stearns's cocktail party." Brent refilled her glass, opened the refrigerator and got himself a beer.

"Martin, Carol Martin, the overweight blond with the short man?

"Overweight? I found her rather voluptuous, curvy."

Joanna smiled, "Yes, I'll give you that. I'd imagine she doesn't lack for partners at these swinger functions."

Brent looked around the room, "So where's our sissy?"

"In the basement, balancing precariously in her six-inch stilettos and locked to the ironing board. She's got two full baskets of ironing including your shirts." Joanna glanced at the clock and did a quick mental calculation. "She'll be ironing for another two hours so why don't you take me to dinner and tell me more about this swinging thing?"

Brent took her into his arms for a deep and lingering kiss. Pulling back he smiled, "That's the best offer I've had all day. Do I have time for a shower?"

"Go ahead. I'll go check on our slut."

Donna turned at the sound of the basement door and the foot falls echoing down the wooden stairs. She shifted on her stilettos, trying to find a position that didn't bring pain to her feet on the cold, unyielding concrete floor. Joanna made her wear the tallest stilettos she owned, six and a half inches high. And while some of her other six-inch 'stripper' heels had platforms that alleviated the strain on her arches, these shoes had no platform. Her feet were torturously crammed nearly vertical into the wicked pointed toes. She felt the pain in her feet, calves and lower back.

Joanna made her entrance and Donna put down the iron and executed the best curtsey she could in her painful heels. Joanna ignored the curtsey but circled, appraising Donna and her ironing project. She walked to the rack of completed ironing and removed a hanger with one of Brent's dress shirts. She held it up to the light and carefully inspected the work. "There's a spot here, from the spray starch." Donna cringed as Joanna pulled the shirt from the hanger, crumpled it up and threw it back in the basket. "Wash and iron again." A pair of pants, a skirt and two more shirts soon followed, accompanied by criticisms about sloppy performance and laziness.

Donna bit her lip and shifted on her stilettos. Joanna's harangue was bringing her to tears. Nearly all of her work, almost an hour of standing in the heels on the hard concrete, was being trashed.

"Bend over," Joanna ordered.

Donna complied, bending at the waist and pulling up her dress and petticoats. She knew what was coming. Out of the corner of her eye she saw Mistress with the cane and she whimpered, frustrated and distraught; *but I'm trying so hard*.

Joanna jerked down Donna's panties and slapped her ass. "Why do you do this? Are you deliberately trying to piss me off? It's ironing, plain and simple; and you can't even do that right. I'm only giving you six with the cane for now. But when Brent and I get home tonight I'll check them again and you'll get six strokes for each piece I reject."

"Thank you, Mistress."

"Sometimes you push my kindness too far."

The first cut of the cane landed and Donna yelped and lurched forward. As she caught her breath she felt Joanna near her and smelled her perfume.

"You are really pissing me off. Hold your position and remain silent for the rest, and I'm giving you two additional strokes. Suffer in silence."

The cane hurt terribly and Mistress Joanna was becoming very adept in its use. Still, the fear of additional cuts of the dreaded cane was enough to make Donna suffer in silence.

For her part Joanna played her victim like a musical instrument. She never let her find a place where she could 'focus' and escape. Joanna attacked high and low, slow and quick, but always with terrifying severity. Donna's knees were shaking at the last two cuts and silent tears and choked sobs racked her body.

Joanna stepped back, returned the cane to its resting place and extended a foot. Donna knelt and kissed Mistress's shoe.

"Thank you, Mistress, for correcting my mistakes and helping me to be a better sissy."

"Up! Brent's taking me to dinner. You'll stay here and finish your ironing." Joanna turned to the wall and removed a pair of ankle shackles. "Put these on."

Donna took the shackles and locked them on her ankles. They were sturdy steel, and the twelve inch length of heavy chain between the ankles effectively hobbled her.

Joanna took another length of chain and locked one end to Donna's right ankle and the other to an eye-bolt set deep in the concrete floor. Pocketing the keys she smiled, "Looks like you have no option but to stay here and iron, so do it right. If you've done a good job you'll be released when Brent and I get back. We might even bring you a doggie bag, since you'll miss dinner." Joanna laughed all the way up the stairs.

Donna wiped away tears of desperation and took a shirt from the basket of ironing.

Brent and Joanna approached the door; they were a striking couple and confident they'd see abundant action at the party. Both were dressed for a hedonistic evening. Joanna wore a simple, but very revealing red wrap dress and red high heels. Tonight she was bra-less and panty-less, her black, seamed stockings held up by a red, lacy garter belt. Brent looked very much the Alpha Male in leather pants and an open front silk shirt that revealed a smooth and massive chest.

Carol Martin, wearing only a short and sheer white robe, warmly greeted them at the door. "So glad you could come, we're looking forward to a wonderful evening." Carol noticed the leash in Joanna's right hand and followed it to the figure standing behind the couple. "And this is…?"

Joanna pulled on the leash and Donna stumbled forward on her five inch heels. "This," said Joanna, her voice dripping with disdain, "is my husband, we call her Sissy Donna."

"Donna," Carol laughed. "Really, and is she here for sex tonight as well?"

"I suppose," mused Joanna, "after a fashion." With a flourish Joanna removed Donna's long coat, revealing her for everyone to see.

By now many of the evening's participants had gathered to see the sissy on display. Donna recoiled at this public exposure and humiliation until the familiar voice calmed her: *I'm a fuck slut. I'm used for other's pleasure.*

Carol eyed the creature before her. Donna was naked save for a small white apron, garter belt, stockings and a balconette bra that exposed her nipples. The most obvious, eye-catching item was the bright pink plastic chastity device and gleaming brass padlock. She fondled the package, testing the weight of it in her hand. Smiling at Joanna she asked, "Is there a key?"

"At home; it's really a rather useless thing, nothing that would serve anyone here tonight."

Carol let the package drop from her hand. "Interesting, yes I see what you meant about the 'sex' tonight."

"Well," corrected Joanna, "I did say 'after a fashion.' Of course she won't be penetrating anyone, not with that thing." Joanna cruelly slapped the chastity device as she said 'thing'. "But she does have a mouth, lips, a tongue and an ass that is open, quite literally, to all here this evening." Donna faced the crowd, "Ladies and gentlemen, for your evening's fucking pleasure I give you Sissy Donna, the wonder slut."

Joanna jerked on the leash and Donna curtsied, bringing howls of laughter from the other guests. Clearly enjoying the humiliation she was heaping on her sissy she continued. "As you can see, she is of no use for fucking," sneered Joanna as she viciously slapped the chastity cage making Donna wince. "But her mouth is always hungry for a cock, her tongue simply loves assholes and pussies, and this tight little ass," Joanna bent Donna over and spanked her ass, "is begging to be filled with cocks and strap-ons. Take a good look ladies and gentlemen; here is your party favor for the night."

Everyone gawked, intrigued by the scene before them.

Joanna grabbed Donna's nipples and cruelly pinched them. "What's your name?" she growled.

"Sissy Donna."

Joanna let go of one nipple and slapped Donna's face. "And what are you?"

"A fuck slut."

With a feral smile Joanna turned to the party guests and gave a 'what did I tell you' gesture. "See, she knows what she is and what she's here for. Her cute little apron is loaded with condoms and lube so please, help yourselves."

A tall woman moved effortlessly through the

crowd; her Kohl-rimmed eyes glaring beneath
short, spiky hair streaked black and red. Her long
arm, tattooed with a snake running its length,
reached out and grabbed the leash hanging from
Donna's collar. "Well, shit, I'll take you up on your
offer." She pulled on the leash, "Down!"

Donna collapsed to her knees, from fear of
her new Mistress or the strength of the arm at the
end of the leash, she didn't know. Her eyes were
locked on the woman's high-heeled ankle boots.

She felt the leash go taut as the woman
walked away. "Come on, slut, I've got some big
cocks you can warm up for me. I want them wet
and hard, but your poor little mouth may never be
the same."

Donna crawled as quickly as possible to keep
up with the strides of her new, long-legged Mistress. She crawled through a maze of bare legs,
bare feet, and high heels and felt the occasional
slap on her ass. The taunts and jeers echoed in her
head: 'Nice of Joanna to bring us a slut.' 'I feel like
a rim job.' 'How about a DP later, cocks in her
mouth and ass?' 'No appetizers for her, only
creampies!' 'I see why Joanna keeps it locked
away.' 'Margo, Dwayne and I want her when
you're finished.'

The tall Mistress waved a hand to acknowledge the last request. "I'll send her over, or
what's left of her." Again the room erupted into
laughter. Mistress Margo stalked down the hallway and turned into a bedroom. Yanking the
leash she directed Donna into a corner. "Wait

there, nose to the wall, and quiet!"

Donna huddled into the corner, glad to be away from the crowd and left alone. She heard voices and movement behind her.

"Turn around, slut!" Mistress Margo ordered.

Donna turned, keeping her eyes to the floor.

"Look up, bitch, time for you to get busy."

She raised her head to see Mistress Margo flanked by two even taller men, one black and one white. Both men were naked and possessed some of the largest cocks Donna had ever seen.

Margo took a cock in each hand and smiled. "Meet Andre and Steve, now crawl over here and pick a cock and get busy. Get it hard in two minutes or I'm gonna kick the shit out of you!"

This Amazon looks like she'd do it, no problem. Donna immediately scurried across the floor on her hands and knees, making directly for the tree-trunk legs of the black man.

Margo grabbed her by the hair and pulled her head up to eye-level with the gigantic cock. "Nice choice bitch. Andre gets hard if the wind fucking blows so it shouldn't take you long. That's the good news. The bad news is that he's nowhere full-sized yet, so you're gonna get a mouthful. Get busy."

Donna stuck out her tongue and licked the bulbous head of Andre's cock when his huge hand suddenly slapped her head, almost knocking her to her knees. "Fuck bitch! Suck it! Get it in your mouth! You know what suck my cock means?" He grabbed her head and savagely pulled it onto his throbbing manhood.

The cock invaded her mouth hitting the back of her throat. This was not the sensual blowjob she would render to Master Brent. This was a brutal face-fucking. She gagged and fought to breathe, but Andre held her fast.

"Not yet, bitch! You start suckin' that cock now or you'll die on it!" He pulled her mouth further down on his magnificent shaft, even when she didn't think she could take more.

As she'd been trained, Donna looked up at her current Master and batted her eyelashes. *Men like it when you suck their cock and look in their eyes. I must use my eyes to show him my pleasure in sucking his cock.* Calmed by these cock sucking mantras, she relaxed and fought back the panic. She ran her tongue over his shaft, and felt the throbbing veins.

Andre relaxed his grip, allowing her a brief respite from the phallic invader. "That's better, bitch, you just got to do it right, yea, oh yeah." He started a slow rhythmic in and out, drawing her mouth up and down the shaft.

Donna flinched when she felt a woman's fingernails rake down her back. "Not too much Andre," Margo said. "I want that cock and that spunk in ME! This little bitch can lick it out when we're done. She's the fucking warm up, the opening act for the star attraction - ME!"

Margo grabbed Donna by the hair and pulled her off Andre's cock. She planted her high-heeled boot in Donna's chest and sent her crashing to the floor.

"I'm the fucking main event here," Margo sneered. She grabbed Andre's cock, "Yeah, hard and wet just the way I like it." She turned back to Donna. "Crawl your sissy ass over there to Steve and get busy with him." Margo pushed Andre to the bed and fell on top of him.

Donna crawled across to the room and found herself in front of Steve as he sprawled in a chair, his legs wide open. He held his cock in his hand, waving it back and forth in front of her face, taunting her. "Do the balls first. I like to have my balls sucked." He slapped her face with his cock, "And no biting."

Performing on instinct created by conditioning she bent to the task and buried her head in Steve's crotch, gently taking one of his balls into her mouth and lovingly sucking on it. *It's good to please men with my mouth.* She moved her mouth to the other ball and reached up to take the cock in her hands. She was totally engrossed now, making love to the cock and balls with her hands and mouth: stroking, kissing, licking and sucking. Steve relaxed and let his head fall back as she gently squeezed a pool of pre-cum from his cock. Her tongue flicked out, kitten like, to lap it up. "Mmm, baby," she mewed, "you taste good." *Men like it when you talk like a slut.* She felt the cock grow and licked up and down its length. With a kiss on the tip she slowly drew it into her mouth.

"Oh yeah," Steve groaned. "That's it, baby."

From the bed came the sounds of frenzied fucking from Margo and Andre. "Don't get him off bitch!" Margo screamed. "He's mine and he's next! Keep it hard!"

Donna did her best to obey, licking and sucking at Steve's mammoth organ and then backing off if she felt him close to relief.

"Oh, oh, yesss," Margo moaned. With a shudder she fell off Andre and gasped. "Get out slut; you can clean up later, when I've got four or five loads in me. Out! Now!"

Donna quickly released her mouth from Steve's cock and crawled from the room. She quietly shut the door, but her respite was brief. As she knelt by the doorway she heard a voice from the living room. "Done in there? Then get your ass in here. We need a condom and a blow job."

Donna entered the living room amidst an orgy in progress. Bodies were everywhere, on the floor and on the furniture. The couplings, or threesomes in some cases, mixed the sexes in wanton free-for-all.

"Over here, slut!" beckoned a large woman with bright red hair and enormous breasts. "Now bitch, get your ass over here! Earl needs a warm up."

Donna reacted instinctively to the command from a superior female and crawled across the room.

The redhead pointed to a man on the floor,

"Get a condom on him and suck him off. I want to ride that cock sometime tonight."

Donna pulled a condom from her apron and looked at the man on the floor. Earl was certainly the hairiest and fattest man she'd seen that evening, certainly nothing like the hunks Steve and Andre she'd already sucked off. But like them, he possessed a large cock. All the men at the party seemed well endowed. *I suppose that's why Mistress Joanna locks me up and has sex with Master Brent. I just don't measure up.*

"Tonight!" screamed the redhead. "I'd like to fuck tonight."

Donna bent down, placed the condom at her mouth, and rolled it down the length of his cock with her lips.

Earl laughed and placed a large hand on the back of her head, forcing her mouth further down his fleshy rod. "Nice trick, bitch, we'll definitely have use for you at our parties."

The redhead began to spank Donna's ass as she sucked Earl's cock "Suck it, cunt! I want it nice and hard."

Earl pumped his rod in and out of her mouth, her lips stretched by its growing length and girth. "Oh yeah," Earl grunted, "yeah, suck it."

The woman roughly pulled Donna away and slowly eased herself onto Earl's cock, grinding her hips into Earl as she descended. She turned to Donna. "Not so fast slut, you're not through yet. Suck his balls while I ride him."

Donna bent to the task, finding Earl's balls

hairier and a great deal more unpleasant than Steve's. But it wasn't her job to make distinctions; *I must pleasure men without hesitation.*

No sooner had she been dismissed than another couple grabbed her. The man had just pulled out of the woman and held his spent and flaccid cock in his hand. He grabbed Donna by the neck, pulled her head to his crotch and wiped his cock clean with her hair.

She submitted to this degradation while the man's lover giggled.

Donna hoped for relief, but knew full well that the evening would bring only despair and more humiliation. She felt her leash tighten once again and crawled away, following the black high heels of the woman pulling the leash. The woman was very short, her high heels making her average height, but she was quite attractive, with a compact body and shoulder-length brown hair. She purposefully led Donna across the room to a leather sofa. The man reclining on the leather sofa was something out of a bodybuilding magazine: rippling and chiseled muscles.

The woman stopped short and jerked on the chain, bringing Donna to her knees. "I brought you something baby. Frank, meet Sissy Donna."

Frank stretched and yawned. "Yea? And what, Diane, do you want me to do with this?"

Diane pulled on the chain, leading Donna into Frank's crotch. "I want you to fuck it. Come on, baby, I've done the girl-girl thing for you. I want to see you take a guy in the ass." She pouted, "C'mon baby, do him, or it, for me, please?"

"I told you, I'm not gay."

"Hello? Alert the media, I fuckin' KNOW that! Look it's not even really a guy." She tugged on the leash, pulling Donna's face into view. "See, does this look like a guy to you? It, she, is a sissy. Just fuck her in the ass, for me, OK, baby?"

Frank stood up, his cock in his hand.

Shit, thought Donna, *it looks like he's holding a club.*

As if Frank could read her thoughts he slapped her face with his cock, poking her with it, rubbing it over her lips. "You want this, bitch; you want this in your ass? You gonna give my lady here a good show? Show me; show me how bad you want it."

Donna didn't even realize she'd opened her mouth until Frank's fleshy pole invaded her gaping cavity. She felt her tongue sliding over its length and closed her lips around it, feeling the texture, the veins pulsing with the blood of lust. She looked up through her long dark lashes, adoring the owner of this most wondrous cock.

Frank paid no heed to her worshipful gaze; he closed his eyes and allowed his shaft to sink further into her mouth. His pubic hairs scratched and tickled her face as she was pulled time and again down his length, burying her head into his crotch.

When he pulled away, she leaned forward to quickly lap up the stream of drool and pre-cum.

Diane shook her head. "What a fucking slut!"

Donna grabbed the massive cock with both hands and took it into her mouth.

Diane stepped in front of Frank and they kissed, trapping Donna between them.

"You better fuck this slut quick. I want you to cum in her ass, not her mouth. Come on, baby, put it in her ass." Diane pulled away from Frank and grabbed Donna by the hair. "On your hands and knees, bitch, open up for my man."

Donna moved into position quickly, catching more cum and drool with her fingers and licking them. *A sissy can never eat enough cum.* She felt Frank move behind her and grab her hips. When she looked up Diane was staring her in the face.

"I've been waiting for him to take a guy in the ass for a long, long time. OK, so maybe you're not a real guy anymore. But you'll do for now. You fuck him back, and make it good." Diane reached down and grabbed one of Donna's nipples, causing her to gasp and moan. "You like that do you? What are you?"

"I'm, I'm a..."

Diane slapped her. "You're a fuckin' whore! Say it!"

Frank buried his cock into her ass as she gasped, "I'm a whore."

"That's right," Diane said, "a fuckin' whore. And what do whores like?"

"A cock?"

"Yea, that's right, you're a fuckin' whore and

you want a cock up the ass." Diane turned and pulled her ass cheeks apart, backing into Donna's face. "Eat my asshole, bitch, tongue me good."

Their attack was relentless. Frank pounded her ass and Diane's ass mauled her face. Donna moaned, squirmed and rocked back to meet Frank's attack; soon the trio fell into a rhythm. The sensations were overwhelming. The relentless ass pounding stimulated her prostate and she leaked out her precious fluid through the chastity device. Donna wept with both frustration and joy as she felt Frank ease out of her. She felt Diane's fingers around her chastity device.

"Lose something?" Diane asked as she held up a gooey finger.

Through tear-stained eyes Donna saw what had to be her own ejaculate, milked from her by Frank's brutal ass assault. Diane brought the finger to Donna's mouth and she opened to receive it.

"Mmm, good girl, there's more," Diane cooed and offering another finger.

Frank grabbed a handful of Donna's hair and wiped off his now-flaccid cock. "You know, baby, that wasn't bad. We need to ask Joanna if we can borrow her some weekend."

Diane squealed and threw her arms around Frank. "Oh, baby, I'd love that! We'd keep her chained up in the basement and feed her nothing but your cum and my piss!"

Across the room Earl watched the scene with great interest. "Now that," he said pointing a pudgy finger at Donna, "has potential."

The big redhead riding Earl's cock reverse-cowgirl style nodded her agreement, "Yea, so put her to work, honey."

Donna lost count of how many cocks and balls she sucked, how many asses and pussies she serviced. Her hair and face were a mess and Joanna hadn't permitted her to bring her purse or any makeup. Party guests wiped their privates on her hair, cleaning themselves with her formerly soft and silken tresses. After an evening as a sex party toy she truly looked like a slut. She was given a glass of water and told to go stand in the corner while everyone else helped themselves to the buffet and drinks.

When the guests decided to use the Jacuzzi the hostess pulled Donna from the corner and led her outside, forcing her to kneel on the hard flagstones surrounding the giant Jacuzzi. She pointed to a stack of towels. "You'll clean the guests before they enter the Jacuzzi."

Donna mutely nodded as she waited for the first guest, a man, to arrive. She reached for a towel and moved to wipe the man's wet and slimy cock and received a slap to the face. "Use the towel AFTER you lick it clean slut!"

Donna licked and sucked the man's cock clean and then wiped him off with the towel. He was followed by another man, and a woman who laughed as she spread her legs. "There must be four or five loads in there, get it all."

When Donna saw the red pumps she immediately knew it was Mistress Joanna who stood before her. "Having fun yet?" Joanna mocked. "I don't know when I've had so much cock; certainly not during our marriage. But I'm making up for lost time; there are several loads down there, so eat up my little darling."

Joanna slid into the Jacuzzi, joined by five other swingers. Brent pulled her close and under the water her hand found his cock. She squeezed it and smiled at him. "It's been a great party."

Brent half-closed his eyes, enjoying both the warm pulsating water and the warm pulsating feminine hand. "They do it nearly every month. Interested in becoming a regular?"

"Mmm, that's something I could get used to."

"Our little Donna seemed to be quite popular; she looks like she's been rode hard and put away wet."

Joanna laughed and released her grip on Brent. "Yes, I must say that Karin and her cage have made a true believer out of me. Though there were moments of hesitation, our little sissy was the perfect slut tonight."

"So capitalize on that." The fat, hairy man stepped over the edge and into the Jacuzzi. "Make it pay for you. Earl Klineman," he extended a large fleshy hand.

"Joanna Barnes," she said, taking his hand.

"Pay for me - how?"

Earl eased his bulk into the water causing it to slosh up the sides of the Jacuzzi. "Videos, I produce adult videos."

"Porn?"

"Adult videos: het, gay, lesbian, some fetish stuff like latex, smoking and BDSM; I'm thinking of expanding into she-males and sissy maids. Your sissy sucks a good cock, she passed the audition," he chuckled.

Joanna and Brent looked at each other, obviously considering the possibilities. Joanna leaned forward, studying Earl's face. "You're serious? What's involved and how much money?"

"Definitely serious and there's not much involved. The money can be good. We shoot these in a day or two. It's not like we have a plot or a script. It will mostly be your sissy dressed up and sucking cock or getting fucked, basically what went on here tonight only I film it and you get a check."

"What do I have to do?"

"I'll send over a contract and I need to have a few pieces of documentation to keep the Feds off my ass."

Joanna beamed. "Our little sissy is going to be in the movies!"

Twenty

When Karin reached for the ringing phone it gave Suzette the chance to take a deep breath. She didn't know how long she'd been secured in Karin's Face Throne, but that moment's relief was much appreciated. Unfortunately it didn't last long as Karin settled back down into her chair, wiggling her bottom 'just so' to seal Suzette's face firmly in the crack of her ass. Suzette's tongue sneaked upwards and inwards as Karin purred and pressed the 'talk' button, "Karin here."

"Hi, it's Joanna, I didn't catch you at a bad time, did I?"

Karin ground her hips and smiled as she felt Suzette squirm below. "No, in fact I'm having a quite wonderful time. How was your swinging weekend?"

"Lovely, Donna and I have never had so many cocks! And that's one of the reasons I called. Evidently she made quite an impression on a producer of adult videos. He thinks I can hire her out for a series of sissy maid and she-male adult videos."

"Really, your little sissy getting it on for the cameras."

"And getting paid for it, or rather the checks will come to me. It seems like a rather sweet deal and I thought I'd call and see if you wanted to make Suzette a star as well."

Karin wiggled her bottom and smiled as Suzette struggled for air. "That *is* an intriguing possibility. Exactly what would our girls be doing, besides each other?"

"Earl, the producer, said it was mostly cock sucking, cum swallowing and ass fucking. Our girls would be little sissy fuck toys that get taken by bigger males and women with strap-ons."

"It sounds deliciously humiliating. Sure, I think we should give it a try, at least once, just to see what it's all about."

"Wonderful," Joanna replied, "I'll take care of everything."

Karin hung up the phone and lifted her bottom, "OK down there?"

Suzette choked out a feeble "Yes, Mistress."

"Good, I want to finish this book." Settling back in her chair Karin wiggled her bottom, pinioning Suzette's head into the specially-built cushion. *My sweet Suzette, a porn star.*

Brent drove the car up the long winding drive; the film shoot was in a secluded location off the canyon road. If the landscaping and huge swimming pool were any indication, whoever was hosting the shoot had plenty of money. He pulled up in front of the house, behind a van where two large bearded and tattooed men were unloading lighting equipment. He stopped the car and turned to his two passengers in the rear seat.

Suzette and Donna sat demurely in back, holding hands as they'd been instructed. Joanna and Karin took great pains to make their 'girls' presentable. For their first film outing they'd dressed them as real sissies, with pink party dresses and yards of crinoline petticoats. They'd given the girls slutty makeup jobs, cute blond wigs and white gloves. Pink, seamed, fishnet stockings enveloped their legs and their feet were crammed into pointy-toed, pink patent pumps with five inch stiletto heels. Each sissy clutched a pink patent purse, which contained the key to their chastity device, just in case the Director might want to do *something* with their precious little sissy clitties.

Ever the gentleman, and perhaps as an extra dose of humiliation, Brent got out of the car and opened the rear doors, offering a hand to help each sissy out. "Be good girls and do everything you're told - and don't forget to swallow." Brent spoke loud enough so that everyone around could hear him. "They'll call me to come back and get you later."

Both girls curtsied to acknowledge their instructions, their actions drawing hoots, catcalls and wolf whistles: 'Hey sweetie', 'Aren't they cute', 'Hey baby, wanna do me?', 'I got somethin' you can swallow.'

As Brent drove away Donna and Suzette stood in the driveway holding hands, unsure what to do, or where to go.

"Over here girls," waved a woman from the patio at the side of the house.

The girls turned and hand-in-hand walked to the woman. Her blonde hair was pulled up and tied behind her head. She wore black spandex leggings and a T-shirt that read '**Keep It Tight for Me, Baby!**' Waving the girls forward she pointed to a cabana by the pool. "I'm Laverne; I'll be doing your makeup and costume. In here, let's take a look at you. So - what, are you - girls?"

Donna and Suzette raised their dresses exposing their chastised sissy clitties.

Laverne laughed and bent for a closer look, taking Suzette's device in her hand, giving it a close inspection. "It's locked on!"

Suzette held up her purse. "Mistress provided the key if it needs to be removed."

"Well shit! This is gonna be one interesting day. Up in the chairs girls, let me fix your makeup and hair. Today you're gonna be French maids." The girls sat nervously as Laverne removed their makeup and applied new product. "Don't get me wrong, you girls looked sweet, but this stuff here has better staying power. That's a good thing when you spend your day under hot lights with your face in a sweaty crotch and get cum facials. You want to look your best don't you?"

In unison the girls offered a feeble, "Yes, Ma'am."

"Ma'am! Shit, you two are just too damned cute." Laverne worked on their eyes, applying long eyelashes heavily coated with waterproof mascara. "Hell, I'm actually gonna have to watch this one today. Either of you ever do an adult video?"

"No, Ma'am, but we have sucked cocks before," Suzette said.

"Have you now? Well, honey, I bet you ain't never seen cocks like these; world-class fuckin' monster cocks that stay hard all day and shoot bucket fulls of creamy cum. You make it through today and *then* you can call yourself a cocksucker."

"These the sissy sluts?" The girls turned to the gravelly voice coming from the cabana entrance. The owner of the voice was a heavyset man, whose bald shiny head had sunburned a bright red. His jeans, faded T-shirt and multiple tattoos were in stark contrast to his very neatly trimmed Van Dyke beard.

"Yea, who the fuck else would they be, shit, look at their pink dresses," Laverne snapped.

"OK, OK, get 'em costume and then into the

kitchen, we're setting up the first shots in there."

"They're chastised."

"What?"

"Their dicks are locked up," Laverne laughed.

"We have the keys," Suzette said.

He shook his head. "They need to do each other, unlock 'em and get 'em on the fuckin' set!" The man turned and walked out.

"He's the director, Rat Dog. These are Rat Dog Video Productions." Laverne began teasing the girls' hair.

"Rat Dog?" Donna asked.

"Not many people use their real names in this biz, honey. What about you?" Laverne finished up with a load of hairspray. "Strip! We need to get you in costume. You girls got workin' names?"

The girls looked at each other and then at Laverne.

"Sissy Donna."

"Suzette."

"Sissy Donna and Suzette, cute and it fits. Hang up your dresses over there," Laverne pointed to a portable clothes rack. "Get into these." She handed them short black maid's dresses very similar to what they often wore at home.

Both girls gave each other a 'so what else is new' look and began to change.

"Unlock those things and get out of those pink shoes." Laverne jerked a thumb at a box, "There's shoes in there, find your size."

The girls quickly removed their chastity devices and took a brief moment to touch parts of themselves for the first time in weeks. Laverne smiled at the sight. "Leave your purses and stuff here, it'll be fine. Come on let's get you on the set."

Donna and Suzette slipped on matching six inch platform stripper heels and followed Laverne out of the cabana and into the house.

They found Rat Dog talking to a well-muscled man in a black silk robe.

Laverne looked at the girls and nodded at the man in the robe. "That's Rex Strong, your leading man."

In one large hand Rat Dog held an expensive professional video camera and with the other he pointed to the kitchen island. "Take one of 'em over that kitchen island."

Rex greedily eyed the girls. "Which one?"

Rat Dog turned to look at Sissy and Suzette, "Doesn't make any difference, you're gonna do 'em both. Do one and then the other. Raven!" Rat Dog called to a stunning brunette. "Do you want to do the strap-on first or get eatin' out first?"

Raven uncrossed her legs, crushed out her cigarette and slid off her stool. Literally gliding across the floor in her stiletto heels she stopped in front of Suzette. "I'll do this one, first she can eat me, then I'll take her in the ass. First time, baby?"

Suzette curtsied. "No, Ma'am, I've been ass fucked before."

"A curtsey? Where'd you get these two?"

"Earl hooked up with a couple at a swing party." He turned to the girls. "Which of you is Donna?"

Donna curtsied and raised her hand.

Rat Dog continued, "Said this one here spent the whole night suckin' cock, eatin' pussy and takin' it in the ass. Hell, they're workin' cheap and supposedly they'll do whatever they're told. OK, people, let's go, I want this in the can by tomorrow afternoon. Fuckin' time is fuckin' money. Kimmy!"

Kimmy appear out of nowhere next to Rat Dog. With her sweatshirt, and glasses she looked out of place on the set of an adult video. In reality she was the Director's Assistant and Script Girl. "OK, the two maids are in the kitchen kissing each other when Raven comes in and she says," Kimmy thumbed through the pages of her shooting script, "she says - 'what are you doing? Now I know why you never get your chores done, you're always fooling around! You want to fuck around? OK, I'll fix that. Steven!'" Kimmy turned another page, "And - OK, Rex comes in and Rex and Raven fuck the maids."

"OK, you two," Rat Dog pointed at the girls, "stand over there by the sink. When I say 'action' you start kissing and fondling each other. When Raven and Rex come in you just do what they want, follow their lead. And make it good, no reason you shouldn't enjoy this."

Donna and Suzette took their positions at the

sink and took each other in their arms.

Rat Dog stepped back and made last minute adjustments to his camera. "OK - ACTION!"

Donna and Suzette leaned into each other, their lips meeting, their tongues intertwining. Suzette ran her hands down Donna's torso, grasping her bottom and pulling her closer, while Donna's hands slid up to Suzette's breasts, slipping inside the low-cut bodice of the maid's uniform. The girls groped and kissed to appreciative nods of the rest of the cast and crew.

Rat Dog moved in close, personally filming the girls' sexual exploration of each other's body. When Suzette brought her hand under Donna's dress to play with her cock Rat Dog zoomed in for a close-up. Satisfied, he slowly pulled back, while at the same time Kimmy pointed a finger at Raven.

On cue Raven strutted into the room. "What the fuck is this? Is this the reason you never get your chores done? What kind of sissy maids did I buy? You want to fuck around, OK, we'll fuck around. Steven!"

Rex walked into the scene coming up behind Raven and taking her in his strong arms. "What is it, baby?"

"It's these fuckin' she-male, sissy maid sluts you bought. They're fuckin' worthless. All they do is play with each other. I say we return them and get our fuckin' money back!"

Laverne leaned over and whispered to Kimmy. "She's off script."

Kimmy nodded. "Yea, a little improv, but it's

OK, it works. This ain't fuckin' Chekov."

Rex picked up his line. "Relax baby, all we need to do is give them a little aversion therapy. Too much of a good thing and they won't want any more of it." Rex grabbed Donna and pushed her to her knees. He let his robe fall to the floor and grabbed her head, pulling it into his crotch.

Donna reflexively opened her mouth and moved toward his growing cock.

Meanwhile Raven slapped Suzette in the face and forced the shaken sissy to her knees. Shedding her skirt Raven towered over the cowering Suzette and lowered her sex onto Suzette's up-turned face. "Suck me bitch, suck me good!"

Satisfied with the size of his erection due to Donna's cocksucking, Rex pulled her up and bent her, face down, over the kitchen island. He lifted her dress, grabbed a handful of vegetable shortening and rubbed it in her ass. "We'll see how much she likes fucking around after this."

As Rex pounded Donna from the rear Raven rode Suzette's face. Rat Dog moved around with his camera, capturing the action from every angle.

Near her own climax Raven grabbed Suzette by the hair and pulled her away. "Like that?" she spat, "you're a fuckin' whore, a sissy maid whore, and now I'm gonna fuck that sissy maid ass. On your hands and knees bitch!"

Suzette turned away from Raven's crotch and fell to her hands and knees, offering herself to the demonic Mistress.

Rat Dog moved to the kitchen island and shot

more of Rex and Donna while Raven donned the eight-inch strap-on. As Raven cinched it tight Rat Dog moved back to capture the impending ass fucking. Raven grabbed a handful of shortening rubbing it up and down the shaft of her dildo and slapping the rest in Suzette's ass crack. "Open up for the lady of the house, bitch."

Suzette howled as Raven rammed her hard. Raven's hands sought out Suzette's nipples and tightly grasped them, using them as anchors for her vicious pelvic thrusts. "Bet you're gonna think twice before you let your chores slide, huh bitch!"

"Oh yes, Mistress," Suzette squealed. "Yes…"

Two hours later they broke for lunch. Laverne took the girls to the bathroom, cleaned them up, and let them enjoy the excellent craft fare. "Get something to eat and then we'll fix your makeup for this afternoon's work.

It seemed that their performance earned them a measure of respect from the rest of the cast and crew and both girls made small talk while they helped themselves to the delicious take-out Chinese food from the craft table.

Stu, one of the grips, was especially curious. "So, you're like what - slaves?"

"Submissives," Suzette answered. "We serve our Mistresses and Masters. We could leave, but we don't. It's who we are, what we want, where we belong."

Donna merely nodded, preferring to let Suzette speak. Much of this was still new to her and Suzette seemed to have a better grasp on it and was better able to talk to people. She picked at her Chinese food, glad for the spicy Kung Pao chicken to take the taste of cum from her mouth.

After lunch Rat Dog set up the second shot, still in the kitchen. He placed the sissies in the center of the room. "OK girls, I'll talk you through this one, just do what I say, follow my direction and we'll loop the dialogue later, ain't gonna be much talkin' anyway. Stu, gimme some diffused lighting, huh?"

"Doin' my best, Dog."

Rat Dog turned to the sissies. "OK, your owners have finished with you and you're cleanin' up the kitchen." He pulled Suzette's arm and pushed her towards the sink. "You stand here, you're doin' the dishes. And you," he pointed to Donna, you're gonna come up behind her." He backed off and looked at the scene through his camera, making the final adjustments. "OK everybody, here we go, quiet! You girls just do what I say."

Suzette put her hands in the sink and Donna stood behind her.

Rat Dog yelled, "ACTION! OK sweetheart walk forward and put your hands on her shoulders, yea, that's it - rub your tits against her back, kiss her neck." He moved to the side to catch the both of them from the side in the same shot. "Grab her tits."

Donna had Suzette pinioned against the sink

and was grinding her tits into Suzette's back. She leaned in to nuzzle and kiss Suzette's neck and Suzette let her head fall back, lost in the moment. In the back of the room several of the cast and crew nodded appreciatively.

"Yea, great, great," said Rat Dog. "Suzi, spin around and grab her, pull her in for a kiss."

Suzette, needing little encouragement, spun around, wrapped her arms around Donna and pulled her in for a kiss. Rat Dog slowly panned up to catch the sissies in full kiss.

Pulling back a bit Rat Dog got the sissies in full frame. "OK, one of you go for the tits, the other for the cock."

Donna dropped her hands and they disappeared under the petticoats of Suzette's dress. At the same time Suzette let her arms slide from Donna's neck to her tits and both sissies began to fondle each other.

"Do it, yea, keep that up, lots of tongue in the kiss. Pull up the dress I wanna see the cock action." Despite his relative bulk, Rat Dog moved like a ballet dancer with the camera, catching every angle while verbally walking the 'girls' through their moves. "Suzi, down on your knees, suck off your sissy sister."

Suzette broke the kiss, gave a sultry shake of her hair and descended like a stripper working a pole, undulating her ass while tracing a line down Donna's body with her hands. On her knees, Suzette threw up Donna's petticoats and grabbed her cock. She leaned forward and kissed the swelling head, then slowly ran her tongue around it. All the while Donna's hands had found her breasts and she furiously pinched her nipples.

Suzette licked her lips, then opened her mouth wide and descended on the cock. After weeks of chastity it was too much for Donna who dropped her hands and grabbed Suzette's head, thrusting her cock repeatedly in Suzette's warm and inviting mouth.

"Do it girls, one of you cum and one of you swallow," coaxed Rat Dog. Even with the sexual energy playing out before him Rat Dog was focused, intent on getting the money shot. "OK, when she cums you take it all in your mouth, but don't swallow, not yet. Hold it in your mouth and then turn and face the camera - and smile."

Suzette's tongue flicked across Donna's cock, and Donna knew she was close to letting go. She grabbed Suzette's head to pull her even closer. With a final thrust, weeks of chastity, teasing and denial sought their release.

Suzette felt Donna reach her peak and knew the torrent was coming. Pulsing jets of milky cum filled her mouth, but she held on, collecting each new stream. Finally Donna slowly disengaged and Suzette felt the limp, slimy cock slide from her lips. Suzette turned to face Rat Dog, held open her mouth and smiled.

Rat Dog panned in, from Suzette's damp face and mussed hair, to her smeared lipstick, and finally to her cum-filled mouth, her pink tongue coated in pearly cum; the money shot. Suzette wiggled her tongue, then lifted it, thick strands of cum slowly dripping back into her mouth.

One of the grips elbowed the man next to him, "She's a fuckin' natural."

"No shit."

"Great, baby, now swallow for me." Rat Dog pulled back for a full-frame face shot as Suzette greedily swallowed the cum and ran her tongue around her lips, getting every last drop. "Cut!" Rat Dog handed the camera to a grip. "Yea, that's good, we'll loop in some moaning and shit later and throw in some soundtrack." He looked at his watch. "We still got good light people, let's get in one more cock-sucking scene, just change 'em around. Laverne, fix their makeup, I want to see if this other one swallows as good as Suzi here."

By the end of the day's shooting, the sissies were well on their way to becoming she-male, sissy-slut stars. Laverne, like a proud mother, cleaned them up, helped them get dressed and fixed their makeup.

Each sissy went home with a contract for a minimum of three more videos and autographed pictures of Rex Strong and Raven. They even posed for Polaroid pictures of themselves sucking Rex's cock and Raven's strap-on, and autographed the pictures for the grips and technicians.

When Brent returned, the girls were back in their pink party dresses and their chastity devices were once again secured. As before he opened the car doors placing them in the back seat where they held hands. "Did you girls have a good day?"

In unison they replied, "Yes, Master."

"Good, your Mistresses will be pleased, both for your performance today and when they get your checks. I understand that Karin is going to host a special viewing party when your video is released. Won't that be fun?"

"Yes, Master." As Brent drove them home the girls sat in silence, clutching each other's white gloved hand, sharing the same thought, *What will they do to us next?*

* END*

"WHAT DO YOU MEAN YOU READ THIS AND DIDN'T GET EXCITED!!??!! READ IT AGAIN SLUT! AND KEEP READING IT UNTIL THAT WORTHLESS SISSY CLIT IS PAINFULLY SWOLLEN IN ITS CAGE.".

READ IT! NOW!

Chatting
with
Constance Pennington Smythe

I actually correspond with my fans and readers. Here are excerpts from various IM dialogues with one of her favorite "girls" the lovely and submissive "E".

Note: These correspondences have been edited to delete any personal information, but otherwise reflect the actual dialogues between Constance and her *girls*.

E: hello Ms Constance

C. P. Smythe: Hello dear.

E: it's so nice to see You

C. P. Smythe: I hope you've been being a good girl.

E: yes Ma'am thank You

C. P. Smythe: I often send my sissy to work in pantyhose and in the winter, when he can wear heavier shirts or sweaters, even a bra. Do you wear something so you can feel pretty all day?

E: sometimes Ma'am. i always wear panties of course. it's quite hot where i am now so i haven't been wearing pantyhose.

C. P. Smythe: Lady Dragon and I are looking forward to your erotic dancing assignment. Given how cute you look in your pictures we just know you are going to come up with some wonderfully slutty items!

E: i look forward to selecting my outfit Ma'am! thank You Ma'am for your compliment

C. P. Smythe: My own sissy loves to dress up. And I love to hear his little heels click-clacking in the kitchen as he prepares and serves the meals and cleans up.

E: oh yes, how high does he wear them?

C. P. Smythe: Personally I never like to see him in anything less than 4". He has some platform 'stripper' heels with a 6" heel and he does quite well in those. He also has a pair of 6.5" heels with 'no' platform that throw his foot into a rather severe position. But he can walk in them, just not as gracefully as his usual 5" heels.

E: that is impressive Ma'am! the highest i have are 5", but i can walk quite well in those Ma'am

C. P. Smythe: My motto for sissies is: the heels can't be too high, the dress can't be too short, the blouse can't be too low-cut and the earrings can't be too long. IMO "too much is not enough."

E: that is a very good motto Ma'am!

C. P. Smythe: Yes, maybe sometime you can send Lady Dragon and I a short video clip of your strutting your stuff for us. Give us 'the walk.'

E: so you like sissies to be very slutty then, oh i would love to Ma'am

C. P. Smythe: I like sissies to be what I want them to be: sometimes a demure 50's housewife, a maid, a stripper, a slut, I even bought a belly dance outfit and a beginning belly dance DVD for my sissy so some day he can entertain Lady Dragon, my Publisher and myself by doing a sexy dance for us.

E: mmm that is wonderful Ma'am, i love to be what i am told to be Ma'am, i adore obeying the whims of a superior Woman

C. P. Smythe: Yes, Lady Dragon and I are working to put together a place where we can all meet and play and find what we need. She is also an author, and a Domme.

E: Giggles! i look forward to meeting her, Ma'am

C. P. Smythe: She also likes to tie up cocks and balls and loves to put tits into bondage and do things to nipples. She has these wicked things she calls 'nipple nails.'

E: ooh, what are those Ma'am?

C. P. Smythe: Something like carpet tacks that she pushes into the nipple and then secures there. Dear, I must run, I have some other business to attend to. But now that we have this connection we should be able to talk more often. Be a good girl and be respectful to all Women. Mistress Constance XOXO

E: yes Ma'am thank you. hope to talk to you later. Curtsies.

E: hello again Ma'am

C. P. Smythe: I imagine that you will be working on your 'assignment' this weekend. All of us are keen to see how you will outfit yourself as a dancing slut. I know my own sissy would go for the classic stripper heels, long gloves, a boa and a fringed and VERY skimpy top and bottom. I could almost guarantee that, sissy is very much the slut at times.

E: giggles, yes I will be working on that this weekend Ma'am! How long is your sissy in chastity for at a time Ma'am?

C. P. Smythe: My sissy wears a CB-3000. Right now he has been locked up for a week since his last release. His longest time was 64 days. Usually I use the plastic, numbered tamper-proof tags, they work quite well. But this last week I've used a small lock. There's just something about controlling that key! "Oh baby, do you want the key? What will you do to get it? Crawl? Beg?"

E: giggles, I have a pink CB2000 Ma'am

C. P. Smythe: Yes, I love the pink ones!! Sissy's next one will be pink. To lock up that little sissy clitty in a pink, plastic prison, that's sexy, oh my! By all means, if you have any sissy friends you may invite them to join our little impromptu group, as long as they are polite and respectful. I'll do my best to give everyone some individual time.

E: Smiles, yes it makes my clitty drip a lot Ma'am

C. P. Smythe: If your clitty is dripping dear wipe it up with your finger and lick it off. I like my girls to recycle. It's fun to feed it to them with a tiny silver spoon, to make it last.

E: mmmm yes great idea Ma'am! Of course I will do that Ma'am, anyway I love it

C. P. Smythe: You're such a good girl. I simply must introduce you to Lady Dragon. **E**: Thank you Ma'am! I would love to meet Her, it sounds like she has a wicked mind Ma'am

C. P. Smythe: We'll make it happen. She's used the sounds on my sissy. That is something he does NOT like. Have you ever had sounds?

E: no I haven't Ma'am, I have seen them being used Ma'am

C. P. Smythe: She inserted the surgical steel rod into his penis, telling him that THIS was how she fucked her girls. She's also put on a strap-on and introduced him to cock sucking, making him gag because "men like to watch a slut take it and gag."

E: oh, I know they do, Ma'am, I have practiced deep throat on a dildo because of that Ma'am

C. P. Smythe: Oh, we are going to have such a GOOD time with you dear. Be a good girl this weekend, but not 'too' good.

E: yes Ma'am! Deep curtsies

E: good morning, Ma'am

C. P. Smythe: Good morning darling. I'm here in the office editing a book.

E: wonderful, Ma'am!

C. P. Smythe: Yes, but I must get back to my own sissy maid book. Yesterday was housecleaning day and my sissy dressed in her blue & white maid's uniform with a cute lace choker, hose and heels and an apron and spent ALL day cleaning MY house. Up and down the stairs in those heels!! Lovely.

E: oooh nice Mistress! what sort of heels?

C. P. Smythe: A pair I bought her, very "maidish" black with a stocky 4" heel and a Mary Jane strap. Not very 'sexy' but very good for a day of cleaning.

E: Oh yes Ma'am very nice

C. P. Smythe: Sometimes I make my sissy wear his heels and then tell him I DON'T want to hear the clicking of those heels so he must walk on tip toes. Ever try wearing HIGH heels and walk on tip toe so the heel doesn't touch the ground? There are so many ways to torment sissies.

E: oh no Ma'am i've never tried that, You have so many great ideas about how to torment us Mistress! if only all Women could be more like You, Mistress

C. P. Smythe: Then you must walk on tip toes in your highest heels this weekend and then write and tell me what it was like for you. Imagine that I am there...watching..."UP on your toes girl, HIGHER...I don't want to hear those heels! Do you understand?" Of course my cane or crop will be handy to correct any mistakes on your part.

E: Yes Mistress

C. P. Smythe: You're such a good girl, so obedient. Oh and do wear that black skirt when you walk tip toe. Mistress loves seeing you in that. And arms held limply at your sides with your wrists turned up, palms down, so pretty.

E: Yes Mistress, thank You!

C. P. Smythe: Darling, my luncheon date is here. Let's hook up later this weekend and you can tell me how you did with your assignment.

E: Yes Mistress, have a great lunch!

C. P. Smythe: Go practice your walking. Mistress Constance

E: hi Mistress- i've been mincing around the house in my purple 5" on tip toe

C. P. Smythe: Good girl! Not easy is it?

E: No Mistress, thank you Mistress. and i am quite sure i look very ridiculous

C. P. Smythe: Oh, but I love the way being on tip toe makes that pretty little bottom sway. The problem is keeping all of my date's hands off!

E: OOOh, i don't mind if they touch Ma'am

C. P. Smythe: Yes dear, I thought you'd like that. A sexy sissy to get my men friends excited.

E: oh yes Ma'am

C. P. Smythe: You'll have to learn how to bend at the waist and serve drinks from a tray...even while you're being fondled and felt up. I expect first-rate service from my girls and they are AL-WAYS available to my guests.

E: yes Mistress, of course!

C. P. Smythe: So, did the walking on tip toes

feel uncomfortable? Not easy is it? Sometimes I make my sissy go barefoot (he HATES that because he SO loves his heels) and I make him walk barefoot on tip toes, like he was on heels, but barefoot.

E: it is hard to do Mistress, definitely, yes it is uncomfortable Mistress

C. P. Smythe: Are you locked up this weekend? Is your clitty locked away?

E: yes Mistress

C. P. Smythe: Mmmm, it must be frustrating to chat with me and have it locked up.

E: it makes me very excited, Mistress

C. P. Smythe: What about discipline? Have you ever been flogged, whipped, cropped, caned, paddled?

E: flogged, cropped and paddled Mistress, a few times

C. P. Smythe: Yes, That's Lady Dragon's realm. She warms you up with a heavy flogger, very sensuous, almost like a massage. But that's only to get the nerve endings alive so they will be receptive to the real pain to come. Then she moves on, to other implements. When you hear Her say "take a deep breath and hold it for Me," you know the worst is coming.

E: owwwww

C. P. Smythe: Mind you, Mistress Constance isn't above blistering a sissy ass with a cane or crop, but I rather prefer more humiliating fare, having you lick the soles of my shoes clean, peeing or spitting in your food, putting things up your sissy bottom, dressing you up.

E: mmmm yes Mistress, this sissy does love the humiliation

C. P. Smythe: Darling, Mistress is going to shut down in the office here and go downstairs for the evening. But I want you to play with your nipples tonight and put something in your bottom...feel how it feels in there because that's the only way sissies get relief. Either they do it, or Mistress milks them, or Master Brent rapes their sissy pussi. But that's how you get your pleasure so I want you to do that for me. Pleasure your bottom and your nipples. You may imagine that Master Brent and I are cuddled up on the sofa, watching you try desperately to make that clitty cream. Give Me a good show...entertain Me.

E: yes Mistress thank you!

E-Mail Role Play

I've also been known to engage in e-mail role play for those who are submissive, respectful and obedient. It's great fun! Here are some real life e-mails between the bubbly and oh-so-submissive "**A**" and myself that include some of this role play. Don't you wish 'you' were a Smythe girl?

C.P. Smythe: I'm delighted you are enjoying our correspondence dear. Your submission gives me great pleasure. I'd love to invite your Wife for tea and have you serve us. Perhaps then she could see what a treasure she has and how much better Her life could be if She fully embraced your submission. Your world would revolve around Her, as it should.

A: Oh Ms. Smythe! *BLUSHING*! i am DEEP-LY and PROFOUNDLY enjoying O/our correspon-dence! i am so honored that You would spend an instant of thought reminding me that You are a real person, and i can only humbly offer that i have not even the slightest doubt. my clitty and my soul tell me that You are as You present: my dream on earth! *blushing*

Thank You so much for every word You spend on me (for Your own amusement) You write so beautifully, You are such an inspiration, You un-lock thoughts in my mind that i did not know were there. You make me blossom.

Oh what a THRILL to serve You and my Wife tea some afternoon, to stand sweetly to the side as You speak with Her, and explain gently, vivid-ly, what pampered life lays waiting for Her to indulge in. And to watch the twinkle of realization grow in Her eyes, to take a few lessons from You and then take me home, to put me to my proper purpose and place. *sissy heart RACING right now!*

C.P. Smythe: If you were here this weekend, when my publisher visits, we'd put wrist cuffs and a collar on you and I'd chain your wrist cuffs to your collar, securing your hands in front of your face. Then I'd place a lovely crystal ashtray in your hands and position you on your knees, con-veniently between my Publisher and me, our own human ashtray holder.

"Spread your legs dear," I kick your thighs apart with the pointed toe of my pump. "That's better," I laugh as I playfully kick your balls and cock cage.

Lady Dragon leans over to tweak your nipple. "He's so well trained, where on earth did you find him."

I blow a stream of smoke in your face and tap my ash in the ashtray directly under your nose. "Let me tell you all about it...."

Note: I'm thinking about inviting your wife over for tea. I can't wait to see the expression on her face when she realizes "who" you are.

"That's...that's my husband!"

I snap my fingers and watch you immediately fall to your knees and begin licking the sole of my high heel. "Yes, your husband - and my maid."

Oh, I have such wonderful and wicked things planned for you.

A: Dear Ms Smythe, You put such wonderful images in my head! ...kneeling, legs kicked wider apart, collared, cuffed, holding Your elegant ashtray just before my made up face. Having made my face up extra pretty, because Ms Smythe and her friends deserve to have as pretty of an ashtray as can be!

Closing my eyes, restraining my reflexive grunt as Your lovely toes impact my distended sissy balls, bulging out from my secure cage. my key one of many in the large silver dish at the front door. When a sissy is granted release, it can take quite a long time to sort out which key is which. And if it takes to long, Mistress's mood may change and retract the offer. Or when She decides time is up, She may simply take whatever key is in hand and find the sissy that belongs to it and grant that sissy relief randomly. It's all up to Her.

BREATHING deeply Your lovely blue smoke as Lady Dragon flatters me so! kneeling painfully, so exposed, vulnerable, as You relate to Her how Your took possession of me. How You found me online and simply encouraged me along my natural course to destiny, learning how eager i was to become a proper sissy maid.

my mind whittled down more and more, until i have no mind of my own at all, more and more of me Yours to use. Dressed and Yours every spare moment of the day, devoted to You and my

Training.

Until one day, as i kneel beside Your table, holding the tea tray, You introduce me to my own Wife! i cannot run, i dare not. my Ms Smythe has not yet been served, nor Her guest. But i feel FULL shame and degradation, dressed in pink satin afternoon service uniform, relieved that it has been washed since yesterday, the copious cum stains no loner evident.

And knowing that it will not me be who explains my predicament, but You. Because i am Your property now. And sensing the arrangement, my wife directs Her questions and interest to You, just as She would if asking a Woman about Her pet doggie.

Thank You so much Ms Smythe!

"YES, I READ THE BOOKS, MISTRESS KARIN AND THE BREAKING CAGE, AND I THOUGHT...WHY NOT? WHY SHOULD I BE BOTHERED WITH HOUSEWORK, SHOPPING, ERRANDS, LAUNDRY AND ALL THE REST?

"LOVERS, WHY SHOULDN'T I HAVE THEM WHEN-EVER I WANT? AND NOW I DO. IT'S ALL ABOUT ME...AND I COULDN'T BE HAPPIER!

"HIM? I THINK HE'S, OR SHE'S, HAPPIER TOO. THE CHASTITY MAKES HIM SO DOCILE AND SUBMISSIVE. HE'S BECOME A WONDERFUL HOUSEKEEPER AND ALL MY LOVERS THINK HE'S THE CUTEST LITTLE THING.

"HE'S IN THE KITCHEN NOW, THE PERFECT LITTLE SISSY MAID WIFE, PROPERLY DRESSED IN HIS WIFEY DRESS, APRON AND HEELS. HE'S MAKING MASTER'S FAVORITE POT ROAST. IT ALWAYS GETS HIM EXCITED TO SERVE MASTER AND I AT ONE OF OUR ROMANTIC DINNERS.

"REALLY, DIANE, YOU NEED TO MAKE CARL INTO A SISSY MAID. FROM LAZY HUSBAND TO PRODUCTIVE SISSY MAID, IT'S A MOVE YOU WON'T REGRET !"

COMING SOON

The third book in the Karin series: The circle of Dominant Women grows as Joanna introduces her friend Simone to the advantages of chastised, submissive, sissy maids. Joanna invites friend Simone and her husband Scott for the weekend, where Gary is outed as sissy maid Donna, and spends the weekend as a sex toy.

Weekend With Friends

by

Constance Pennington Smythe

"*He really does anything* you say?" Simone asked incredulously.

Joanna nodded and smiled, slowly drawing out her reply, "Anything."

The two friends and work colleagues were enjoying a glass of wine on a Friday evening. As they drank they discussed men and relationships, the talk becoming bawdier as the grape was consumed: *in vino veritas.*

"Yes, he's been my total submissive for quite some time now. I am the Goddess and he is my slave. I am a woman of total leisure and supreme head of the house." Joanna made the statement matter-of-factly.

Simone took another sip of wine and placed her

glass on the table. "Damn, no wonder your house is so clean and you have all this free time. You make him do everything?"

"Actually I really don't have to 'make' him do much at all. At this point, he's so pussy-whipped I only 'make' him do things to see him squirm. But it is fun to try to find new ways to push his buttons."

"What about sex?" Simone asked.

"Hell, I get as much as I want, when I want it, the way I want it, although it's almost never penetrative sex, at least from him. No, I'm afraid his little 'thing' has pretty much been reduced to an implement of torment and frustration for him."

Simone shook her head in amazement.

"I've got his little wanker under lock and key," Joanna continued. "I really don't need it and he can't get to it."

"You don't!" Simone said.

Joanna smiled, reached into her purse and fished out a small key on a golden chain. She held it out to Simone. "If I dangled this in front of Gary he'd be down on his knees in a second, waiting to do whatever I demand."

Simone shook her head in disbelief and drank the rest of her wine. "Really?"

Joanna nodded, "Really."

Simone cautiously eyed Joanna and leaned in closer. "So, uh, what kinds of things do you, uh, do - exactly."

Joanna laughed. "Shit, Simone. Don't you ever cruise stuff on the web, read Variations, Penthouse Letters, play little sex games?"

Simone shifted nervously in her chair. "Well, yea, I

mean, Scott and I have seen some videos and sometimes he buys these magazines and, and - I mean damn, Joanna; you're talking the real shit, right?"

Joanna narrowed her eyes over the top of her wine glass and deliberately nodded at her friend.

Simone sat back in her chair and sighed. *What's this all about? Where is this all going?* Another question obviously on her mind, she studied Joanna. "So, are you like, a, a Dominatrix?"

Joanna reached into her purse for a silver cigarette case and languidly placed a cigarillo in a holder. "If you're asking me if I dress up in leather and high-heeled boots and carry a whip and a riding crop, yes. If you're asking me if I put Gary in bondage and beat him, yes. If you're asking if I fuck him in the ass with a strap-on and put nipple clamps on him, yes."

Simone stared, wide-eyed.

Joanna took a drag from her cigarette and expelled a sensuous stream of smoke. "The idea excites you, doesn't it?"

Simone leaned back as if trying to maintain some space from Joanna. "Well, I mean, yeah. I never really knew any body that actually did that kind of stuff, or at least admitted to it."

Joanna reclined in her chair and studied her friend. There was a moment of awkward silence while Simone played with her wine glass and Joanna finished her cigarillo.

Joanna leaned forward and purred, "Would you like to see it? Would you like to watch Gary submit to us, to crawl and kiss our feet?"

Simone felt the wetness in her sex; the idea did

excite her. Hell, Scott read his damned porno mags and sometimes they rented 'fuck-me-suck-me' videos, but sex didn't seem to be as exciting these last few years. Yet, here was her friend Joanna, a good ten years older, and having a great sex life; a life that Simone could not imagine. *Yea, why not* she thought, *what's the harm in just checking it out*? Simone tried to be nonchalant, "Sure, I'd like that sometime."

Joanna cocked her head, "Now?" she asked.

Simone lost her composed façade. "What, you mean now? Tonight?"

Joanna shrugged her shoulders in a 'why not' gesture.

Simone felt warm. Was it the wine or the steamy topic of conversation? The kids were out doing some Friday night activity and Scott was off doing who knows what. She was out with Joanna because she had the early part of the evening free, so why not? She regained her composure enough to say, "Yes, Joanna, I'd be very interested to see what you are up to. You surprise me, you really do surprise me."

Joanna reached across the table, smiled and reassuringly took Simone's hand. "You won't regret this. It will be fun." She signaled the cute young waiter for the check.

"SEE, WHAT DID I TELL YOU?"

"HE'S ACTUALLY ON HIS KNEES, CRAWLING TO US."

"WELCOME MISS SIMONE PROPERLY, KISS HER FEET."

"HE'S REALLY DOING IT, HE'S KISSING MY FEET!"

"THAT'S ONLY A SAMPLE. HE'LL DO WHATEVER HE'S TOLD. HE'S QUITE OBEDIENT, QUITE WELL-TRAINED. PUT YOUR HANDS ON THE FLOOR. NOW BEG SIMONE TO STEP ON YOUR HANDS WITH HER HIGH HEELS."

"OH I LIKE THIS, I CAN FEEL HIS HANDS UNDERNEATH MY FEET. FEEL THAT, BITCH!"

"GO AHEAD YOU CAN DO IT HARDER, HE'S NOT EVEN CRYING YET."

COMING SOON

Female Domination Short Stories

By

Constance Pennington Smythe

It's the first collection of Female Domination short stories published by erotic author Constance Pennington Smythe. Enjoy the powerful and erotic world of Female Domination and male submission with these new stories and favorite themes: Chastity, Cuckolding, Mini Men, Suburb Submissions and more, all featuring Dominant Women and the submissive men in their lives.

Turn the page for a preview of *A Visit to Smythe Stables*, just one of the many offerings to be found in this new work.

A Visit
To
Smythe Stables

Welcome to Smythe Stables
A Division of
Smythe Domination, Ltd.

Tours and milking parties by appointment only.
Family visits by appointment only.
Pony cart races every Saturday.

Visit our gift shop complete with a wide array of
milking videos and milking accessories.

Custom-made milking videos of your husband,
boyfriend or son available.

Ask about our sissy cream delivery service. Fresh
spunk delivered to you daily to use in feeding your
sissy maids.

Note:
Males are forbidden to walk upright.
Males may only speak when spoken to.
Do not feed the males.
Males do not have names, only numbers.
Please DO handle the males.

by
Constance Pennington Smythe

A Visit
To
Smythe Stables

Chapter ONE

The gravel crunched under the tires as the black and white chartered bus, its tinted windows hiding the occupants inside, made its way up the winding drive. Passing a green fenced in pasture and a wooded area it slowed to a stop in front of the imposing red and white building. It was a long, low and windowless structure with several sliding doors along one side; the sign in the front, Smythe Stables, was the only clue as to what might be inside. With a hiss, the doors of the bus folded open.

A tall austere woman rose from her seat at the front of the bus and turned to face her young charges. Her height was enhanced by the gleaming black stilettos, and the long, sheer nylon covered legs that extended from her black leather pencil skirt. She moved effortlessly on the wicked high heels as she walked down the aisle of the bus. Looking back at her were row after row of feminine faces, this year's graduating class from Lady Caroline's Academy for Young Ladies.

"Today is the practical exercise in the milking of the submissive male. We've covered the theory and physiology in the classroom. Here you will put the theory into practice. Your future husbands will need to be regularly milked. Whether or not you do this or assign it to someone else, it is important to knowledge of the practice. It is my recommendation that either you, or your Alpha Male lover perform this service on your husband. Such personal 'attention' is more humiliating to the male and drives them further into submission. Ms Constance Pennington Smythe has made her milking stable available to us, very generous of her. She will host an afternoon tea for us at her club, and then we will return to the stables for the strap-on exercises before we depart. Are there any questions?"

A beautiful girl with flowing blond hair raised her hand. She was dressed in the same uniform as her classmates: a crisp white blouse, sheer stockings, bracelet-length kid leather gloves, a tartan mini skirt and high-heeled court shoes. "Where do all the males inside come from?"

Lady Caroline slipped on her black leather suit coat. "Disciplinary problems, males who couldn't be trained or perform to standards. A few languish here simply because their owners tired of them and at least here they can serve some function." She turned to look at a pretty brunette. "Susan, I believe your father is inside."

Susan smiled and nodded. "Mother sold him to Ms Smythe. He was getting in the way, wasn't good for sex, a premature ejaculator Mom said, and wasn't making a good domestic. We have a really good sissy maid now and Miguel is a better lover for Mom."

The girl in the seat in front of Susan turned around. "Your Dad's in there? That's fuckin' cool."

Her outburst brought instant recrimination from Lady Caroline. "Deidre, mind your language!"

"Yes, Ma'am."

"Remember girls, domination and superiority are not crass; wield your power and authority in a regal and ladylike manner. When we go inside you will each pick out a slave. Warders will be around to provide you with gloves and lubricant and show you how to hook the suction nipple to their penis. The males have not been milked for several days so should be very amenable to our attention. But to help them along everyone add a spritz of scent."

Twenty five gloved hands disappeared into twenty five identical and fashionable clutches to remove bottles of expensive perfume. In an instant the bus filled with a sensual aroma.

The male bus driver, naked and gagged with a large penis gag, breathed in the heady scent and felt his cock try to stiffen in its chastity cage. The sharp spikes inside the device brought immediate pain and put down any attempts at erection.

Caroline returned to the front of the bus. "When you get inside, remember YOU are the superior Female. This is your last semester at my academy. You're all of legal and marriageable age and when you graduate you will enter the world to search out and cull those submissive males from the herd. It won't be difficult. Society abounds with them, and I and my faculty have provided you all the skills and tools you need to capture a husband and to staff your households with sissy maids. But to obtain maximum efficiency from male slaves you need to know about their care and feeding. So pay attention today, these are valuable lessons. Please form up outside the bus and wait for me."

The girls walked down the aisle, each one stopping to tighten their leather gloved hand into a fist and deliver a hard blow to the bus driver's right arm and shoulder. His arm was covered in black, blue and greenish bruises that never healed. Chained to his seat there was no way he could escape, even if he wanted to. But he'd accepted this for so long that although they hurt, he sat and took his beatings, offering whimpers of pain into his penis gag. The girls, for their part, delighted in seeing who could force the loudest wails from his gagged mouth.

Caroline watched this ritual with amused detachment. *At this rate he'll only be good for another year before that right arm is useless. Oh well, I'll sell him to Constance and he can spend the rest of his days inside the stables.* Before leaving the bus she took the remote control from her pocket and pressed "medium." The steel balls inside the driver's butt plug began to gyrate and bounce against one another. She smiled as the driver squirmed at the anal invasion. Grabbing his wrists she brought them to his neck, locking the cuffs to his collar.

He looked at her; his eyes begging and pleading for mercy. He knew there was no mercy, never had been, never would be. But something deep inside of him still searched for what he knew he'd never find.

She saw the look, reached down and viciously pinched a nipple. *Eventually that look will be gone; he'll be destroyed, resigned to his fate. But I do like them like this, ever hopeful...right before they're completely broken.*

She left the bus and joined her fresh-faced entourage: so prim, so proper, so perfectly dressed and coifed. And so full of malevolent evil, carefully inculcated by her, "Follow me girls."

Mistress Karin

Constance Pennington Smythe

What happens when a man gets his wish to be submi-sisve? What happens when a woman embraces her domi-nant self? For Karin Calloway and her hapless husband, otherwise known as her maid Suzette, it becomes an erotic power exchange that gives them both what they desire. Is Suzette destined to become a cuckolded sissy maid? What new humiliations and torments will Karin and her evil friends, Trudi the German dance instructor and socialite Sheila Remington, visit on poor Suzette?

Published by Romance Divine LLC
ISBN 978-1-934446-11-9

Enjoy an excerpt from:

Mistress Karin

By

Constance Pennington Smythe

𝒦arin used a small piece of toast to wipe up the egg yolk on her breakfast plate. Without looking, she held out the morsel of food and felt it gently removed from her hand. She didn't have to see the scene unfold to know what happened. These small offerings had become valued treats for Suzette.

On some mornings Karin snapped her fingers and pointed to the floor. Suzette immediately knelt beside her Mistress, hoping that her bland diet might be augmented by those few precious scraps of 'real' food. Since her submission her diet had been meager at best. The morning gruel, often flavored with cigarette ashes, Mistress's 'nectar' or spit was supplanted by a wretched concoction called *Prison Loaf.* Karin discovered the loaf during a web search and it now formed the basis of Suzette's second meal of the day. The loaf was a mixture of grated carrots, wheat bread, artificial cheese, spinach, beans, and raisins – among other items. It was unappetizing, and purposely meant to be. That's why Suzette would literally sit and beg for table scraps.

Karin idly turned the business pages and sipped her coffee. "How long since you've been to the office?"

"Maybe two months, Mistress?" He phrased it as a question, he truly didn't know.

She didn't press the issue, content with his answer. It was what she wanted – his isolation from the world at large – total focus and dependence on her. He was kept busy all day with chores, tasks, dance lessons, aerobic workouts in cute pink leotards. He was denied computer and television access, she'd locked those out. Newspapers were forbidden to him, but he was allowed women's magazines: *Vogue*, *Good Housekeeping,* and *Glamour*.

"Three months," she said. "It's been three months since you had your –'breakdown' – and had to take time off from work. But I've been able to fill in nicely for you; after all, Daddy did leave the company to me."

"Yes, Mistress, but I thought –"

"Wrong! You thought wrong, and that's why I'm doing the thinking now. You thought that the executive with the perfect wife was the ideal. And I agree with you." She waited, wondering if that statement meant he would think they were going back to the old way; he as the CEO and she as the trophy wife. A slight smile crossed her lips as she watched his eyes light up with that hoped-for realization. She'd grown to love these moments, watching as he rose to the bait and savoring his utter desolation when she pulled out the rug and crushed his hopes. *If only his hopes were some kind of living, organic thing that I could crush with my stiletto, feel the spike heel puncture it, watch the life force slowly drain away.*

"One of the girls from the office will be coming by today." She looked him in the eyes; she wanted to remember this moment – and his reaction. "They'll be bringing papers for you to sign, your resignation."

He started to talk, even though he knew he didn't have permission. When Karin held up her hand he quickly shut his mouth.

"You will resign from your position as CEO. You will sign over all of your shares and interests in the company to me. Furthermore, you will sign over all other assets, financial and material, to me." The shock on his face, the fear, it was priceless. "You will sign a general power of attorney giving me complete control over you.

"Yes, we are going to have the perfect corporate marriage. I'm going to be the powerful, high-priced executive. And you, you my little slut, will be the trophy wife, or, in your case, the trophy sissy maid husband. As the executive I'll have trophy lovers, and you will serve them as you do me."

His shoulders fell and his chin dropped to his chest. Karin was surprised at how easily he yielded his manhood to her. She'd now taken everything, reduced him to a servant in her house. "You will sign all the papers put before you."

He meekly nodded, "Yes, Mistress."

She held out a piece of bacon and watched as his eyes lit up and he gently took it between his lips. *I destroy his career, his marriage; take his freedom and his manhood, and a scrap of bacon makes it all better.*

Karin visualized her basement project: the cage, computer, restraints and accessories. Her experiments with operant conditioning and behavior modification worked with Steven; maybe she was on to something.

She rose from the table and walked to the foyer, her husband crawling obediently at her side. "You have your list of chores. And spend thirty minutes practicing walking with the book on your head. Wear your five inch heels; work on that posture and taking the short and dainty steps. There will be times when you won't be crouching and short so you're looking up to women. I may want to pimp you out as a tranny, fetish runway model." She laughed at the thought; Steven, now Suzette, in stilettos, strutting the catwalk and shaking his submissive ass to the gathered throng.

"Be sure to sign all the papers this afternoon. I want this over, behind us, so we can move on. There's no going back." She looked down to see her husband on his knees, planting loving kisses on the toes of her stylish high heels. *No arguments, he simply accepts his situation...amazing. What started out as sex games, a little B & D...* "You'll still be my husband; you'll still keep your cock and balls, although that cock will seldom be out of chastity. And when it is, I can guarantee you won't enjoy it and you'll beg to lock it up. I don't want you to ever forget what you were...or how far you've fallen."

She reached down and patted him on the head. "This really is best, for both of us."

His eyes met hers; he nodded his agreement and returned his lips to her shoes.

Karin arrived at the office, her office, the seat of her new empire, in good spirits. She felt free, even though she was still – technically – married.

Laurel, her secretary, greeted her with coffee and the preliminary financials for the newest corporate venture. "You have a meeting with Acquisitions at ten-thirty and a presentation from Product Development at two." With the grace of a relay baton hand-off Laurel exchanged the coffee in her hand with Karin's purse. "I watched him, oh 'her' – sorry – on the monitor. She cleaned up in the kitchen and went to change for her aerobics."

"Thank you, I have some papers for you to take to my house today." Karin settled into her leather chair and held the coffee cup with two hands. *Life is good.* "Take Sharon with you, she's a Notary isn't she? Make sure my little slut signs them all, you witness and Sharon can notarize."

"Yes, Ms. Calloway." Laurel turned to hang up Karin's coat. "Do you think we might be able to – I mean if it's OK with you – maybe we could –

"You want a play date with my sissy maid." Karin sipped her coffee and placed the cup on her desk. Certainly Laurel was competent and efficient, but had Steven hired her for her physical attributes, some latent submissive tendencies he possessed? At five-ten, and in her four inch heels, Laurel would have towered over Steven. Her blonde hair and blue-eyed beauty would have enthralled any man. "Like what you've been seeing on our office webcams?"

"It's awesome."

Karin chuckled. Laurel was a good fifteen years younger than her so 'awesome' was probably high praise in that age group lexicon. "He knows that we've been watching him from the office, but he's never been put on real-time, personal display. It might be good for him. And for you and Sharon to show up, his former secretary and Chief of Administration, think how humiliating that will be. Yes, have a good time, put him through his paces as it were. Did he ever forget Secretary's Day?"

"We call it Administrative Professional's Day, but yea, we'd have to remind him and then he'd just tell us to order ourselves some flowers."

Asshole. Karin shook her head. *He probably had them order the flowers for our anniversaries and even shop for the gifts. Well now the flimsy lingerie would still be bought, but worn by the true slut of the house.* She smiled at Laurel, *might as well get them trained right.* "Have a good time; it's your chance for a little revenge. But I want pictures and video, and I want him to know you're taking them and why."

"Yes Ms. Calloway, we'll take good care of him – uh- if you know what I mean. And he never, I mean Steven –

"Suzette."

"Yes, Suzette, she never came on to me or any-thing, tried anything sexual. Maybe he wasn't always the most considerate boss, but –

"Laurel, trust me, I understand. If he did want to

get into your panties...it's because he wanted to wear them." Karin saw something in the young secretary's eyes. "What?"

"Oh, it's just that last year...I had this new pair of heels; I saved for three paydays and had them in my desk drawer and then one morning – they were gone."

Both women shared a knowing moment and then turned their attention to the monitor where Suzette, resplendent in a pink leotard, was bouncing to her workout video.

"Payback time," Karin said.

Laurel smiled at the flouncing sissy maid on the screen. "Payback time."

Suzette put away her workout DVD and went to shower and change her clothes. She knew that every room was equipped with cameras and that Karin, and possibly others, were able to monitor her every move. Under Karin's regime even the shower ritual was feminized; shaving of all body hair, washing with scented soaps, exfoliating and moisturizing. Suzette wrapped a towel around her middle, tucking it in at her bosom. A second towel went around her head, turban style, while she carefully plucked and tweezed her eyebrows into an arch. She finished her shower regimen by moisturizing her legs and using a hair dryer to blow-dry the area around her chastity device.

Suitably exercised and cleaned she donned her daily maid uniform of black dress, garter belt and stockings, bra and black pumps with five inch stiletto heels. Working makeup consisted of eyeliner, mascara and lipstick. It was Karin's decision when more make-up was warranted.

Suzette's heels clicked along the tile floor as she made her way to the living room. From the book shelf she selected a book suitable for her walking exercise. Just in case someone was watching, or might view a recording later, she turned and curtsied to the camera mounted in the ceiling corner. She carefully placed the book on her head and then let her arms fall slowly to her sides, elbows in, forearms out and wrists hanging limply. Carefully she stepped out, her back straight, taking small steps, one foot in front of the other, heel-toe, heel-toe. She made it to the end of the room and executed a slow and cautious turn, but the book slid from her head. Her reflexes were good; she caught the book and placed it on top of her head. Before starting across the room again she glanced at the mantle clock. *It hasn't even been two minutes, almost, almost twenty eight to go.* Suzette hated these tiresome and monotonous drills, book balancing and curtsey practice. They were mindless and it made it hard to concentrate. And yet Karin seemed to know when she was slacking in her efforts and she was punished. *OK, focus, we need to get this over with – concentrate – balance – posture.* She stepped out again; *back straight, titties out, sissy wrists and sissy steps.*

Sharon leaned over Laurel's shoulder to get a better look at the monitor. "How many times has he dropped the book?"

"Four," Laurel said. "And Ms. Calloway wants us to call him her, or she."

"Well, her, him, it, she, slut...whatever. With these papers," Sharon held out a black leather portfolio, "she's fucked – big time."

"Yea?"

"Oh yea, once she signs, you witness and I notarize, it's all over. Our little sissy slut's got nothing; Karin's got it covered, signed sealed and delivered." Sharon stood and tucked the portfolio under her arm. "So, go to lunch and then go seal the fate of our former boss?"

Laurel clicked off her computer, "I can't wait."

Suzette feared the daytime doorbell. It was never good news; if it wasn't Miss Trudi it was something equally painful, degrading or humiliating. Karin controlled access to the house so any visitor came with her approval, and must be properly greeted – and obeyed. She jumped at the first ring, but quickly composed herself and walked to the door; *It's probably those papers I was supposed to sign.* Her trepidation was well founded as she opened the door and saw two former employees.

Sharon and Laurel stood at the door. Their faces showed no surprise, having witnessed Suzette's performances on the web-cam feeds at their offices.

"Slut!" Sharon took control, ever the efficient Administrative Supervisor. Shorter than Laurel, and more full-figured, Sharon possessed an authoritative air that must have always given Steven an office thrill. "Are you going to invite us in?"

Suzette executed an automatic bob curtsey. "Yes, sorry Sharon –

The hand hit his face with a resounding SLAP, jerking his head around and sending a clip-on earring flying across the room.

"MISTRESS SHARON," she growled as Sharon pushed past him into the foyer.

Laurel followed behind, unable to control her laughter. "You asked for that one. Best to remember who you and who WE are." She plucked a cane from the umbrella stand as she walked by.

"Yes, Mistress Laurel." His hand stroked his cheek and he stole a glance in the mirror. *She may have given me a black eye.*

Laurel slashed the air with the cane, "Wicked."

"You know how to use that?" Sharon asked.

Laurel giggled and shook her blonde hair, "No."

"On-the-Job training?" Sharon laughed. "Somebody might get hurt."

"You think?"

Suzette quickly turned to follow the women as they went to Karin's home office.

Suzette watched Sharon sit in Karin's desk chair while Laurel relaxed in a wingback chair in the corner, menacingly tapping the cane on the footstool.

Sharon began removing a sheaf of papers from

her briefcase. She was focused on organizing the papers and didn't even look at Suzette. "Do you think we might get some drinks? What do you think Laurel, our little slut seems a bit slow in the service area."

"Absolutely, I remember how he – oh, she – used to be when she was our boss: "where's this, get me that, I need –

"Sorry Mistress Sharon, Mistress Laurel – uh – what would you like?" Suzette performed her best and deepest curtsey.

"Coffee," Sharon said.

"Diet Cola," Laurel said. She grabbed a book from a nearby end table. "Over here slut." Laurel waited while Suzette approached and curtsied. "Put this book on your head and keep it there while you bring our refreshments. We watched your efforts earlier and you need practice."

"Yes, Miss Laurel."

"And ice cubes," Sharon finished with her papers. "Bring a bucket of ice cubes."

Both women laughed as Suzette curtsied, placed the book on her head, and carefully walked from the room.

"Can you believe we used to work for that twerp, rush to get his coffee, pull a file or make copies?" Sharon shook her head. "I always felt there was something; I just couldn't put my finger on it."

"I used to catch him looking at my feet," said Laurel, "thought he had a foot fetish, but I think he wanted to wear my shoes." She removed a digital camera from her purse, "Karin said she wanted pictures. I guess the high heel is on the other foot now."

PLOP! Both women smiled at the sound of a book hitting the kitchen floor and the scurrying of stilettos on tile.

Within minutes Suzette appeared. She held a silver try with a coffee service, a Diet Cola and a bucket of ice cubes.

"Turn around, look at me," ordered Laurel. "Ms. Calloway wanted pictures, something about the employee newsletter?"

"Give us your best curtsey," Sharon teased, "hold it, smile and look at the camera."

Suzette did her best to curtsey while holding the tray – and smiling – but the fear and shame were evident. She blinked at the camera flash and almost dropped the tray.

Laurel selected 'play' on the camera to look at the picture. "Perfect, what a total sissy you are. Now serve Sharon her coffee and bend over so we can get a nice view of your cute panties with the ruffles. Oh and be sure and turn to look at the camera. We want everyone to know it's you – Sissy Suzette." The women let Suzette serve each one of them and then ordered Suzette to place the try on a table.

"Over here," Sharon pointed to the floor by her chair. "We need to take care of Ms. Calloway's paper work – before we take care of you." She looked at Laurel. "How many times did he drop the book?"

"Five times on the video and once a few minutes ago."

"Six, very well. Take six ice cubes slut, and stick them up your sissy ass."

For a moment Suzette remained frozen in place,

but another stinging SLAP from Sharon had him reaching for the ice cubes.

"Turn around," ordered Sharon, "We want to watch. Laurel, get some pictures of this. Six, and shove them all the way in your sissy pussy - slut. Face the camera...smile, show everyone how much you like having that little hole filled."

The women laughed and jeered as Suzette gingerly inserted six ice cubes up her ass.

"Cold?" mocked Sharon.

"Y-y-y-es, M-m-m-istress."

"Not our problem. Kneel; you've got papers to sign. You've served us refreshments, now you'll serve up something even more precious for Ms. Calloway, your life."

One by one Sharon handed papers down to the kneeling sissy maid.

"This signs over all your finances and puts all the accounts in Ms. Calloway's name only. This deeds all material possessions to Ms. Calloway, and a General Power of Attorney giving all rights and decisions to Ms. Calloway."

Suzette knelt and tried to sign, but was shaking from her ice-filled ass.

"Too cold?" teased Laurel.

"Yes, Mistress."

"Do you want to take one out?" Her voice now had a more honeyed tone.

"Please, Mistress, yes, oh please."

"OK, one, you may remove one. Squeeze it out; make us a little icy poopsicle."

Suzette reached behind her, squeezed her buttocks and caught the piece of ice in her hand. Her relief was short-lived.

Sharon, squeezed her embossing seal on the first document. "Put the ice cube in your mouth."

Suzette turned to Sharon, who continued with her paperwork, ignoring the kneeling sissy. "Mistress? You mean –"

The cane landed with a stinging blow, very high on the buttocks. There was the first searing pain, and then that second bloom of deeper pain. Suzette shrieked.

"Put the fucking ice cube in your mouth!" Laurel struck with the cane again, this time leaving a nasty welt on Suzette's shoulder. She drew the cane back for a third blow as Suzette popped the ice cube in her mouth. "That's better. You need to learn to do what you're told. Does your ice cube taste yummy?"

Suzette shook her head, her face showing the distaste of the ice cube, and tears streaming down her cheeks from the wicked cane.

"So the rest of the ice cubes can stay in your ass?"

Defeated, Suzette nodded. She was totally humiliated by women she used to supervise, her sphincter felt frozen and her ass and arm stung from the cane.

Laurel backed up to take another picture, "Look at the camera and smile. Say 'I'm a happy sissy slut'."

"This one is a personal services contract saying that you will provide domestic services for as long as Ms. Calloway deems necessary." Sharon handed down yet another paper and Suzette signed while the camera flash lit up the room.

Recommended Reading

There many books on the topics of Female Domination, BDSM, Cross-Dressing and other aspects of the alternative lifestyle. The following are a few from the current canon on the subjects and are recommended reading for a woman who wants to learn more about this lifestyle. This list is by no means complete, but these are works with which I have personal familiarity.

<u>Female Domination</u>

Female Domination: An exploration of the male desire for Loving Female Authority © 2003 by Elise Sutton

The Art of Sensual Female DOMINANCE: A guide for Women © 1998 by Claudia Varrin

The Sexually Dominant Woman: A Workbook for Nervous Beginners © 1998 by Lady Green

The Mistress Manual: The Good Girl's Guide to Female Dominance © 2000 by Mistress Lorelei

The Training and Education of a Husband Vol. I © 1996 by Patricia de Gifford

The Training and Education of a Husband Vol. II © 1996 by Patricia de Gifford

Sex Tips from a Dominatrix © 1999 by Patricia Payne

Sissy Maids

A Charm School for Sissy Maids © 2001 by Mistress Lorelei

Training With Miss Abernathy: A Workbook for Erotic Slaves and their Owners © 1998 by Christina Abernathy

Miss Abernathy's Concise Slave Training Manual © 1996 by Christina Abernathy

Cross-Dressing

*Miss Vera's Finishing School for **Boys** Who Want to be **Girls*** © 1997 by Veronica Vera

Miss Vera's Cross-Dress for Success © 2002 by Veronica Vera

BDSM

Screw the Roses, Send Me the Thorns: The Romance and Sexual Sorcery of Sadomasochism © 1995 by   Philip Miller and Molly Devon

Learning the Ropes: A Basic Guide to Safe and Fun S/M Lovemaking © 1992 by Race Bannon

Recommended Web Sites

Don't forget the search capabilities of the world-wide-web.

Female Domination

www.elisesutton-homestead.com

www.akashaweb.com

www.femdomdestiny.com

Cross-Dressing

www.crossdresslasvegas.com

www.glamourboutique.com

www.pierresilber.com

www.xdress.com

Chastity

www.keptforher.com

www.cb-2000.com

www.tpe.com (Chastity info via the Altarboy link)

www.chastitylifestyle.com

www.chastitymansion.com

About the Author

Constance Pennington Smythe

Constance Pennington Smythe is an erotic author. She is retired from the corporate world, has lived abroad, possesses multiple degrees, has been an adjunct professor, and is multi-lingual.

www.cpsmythe.com